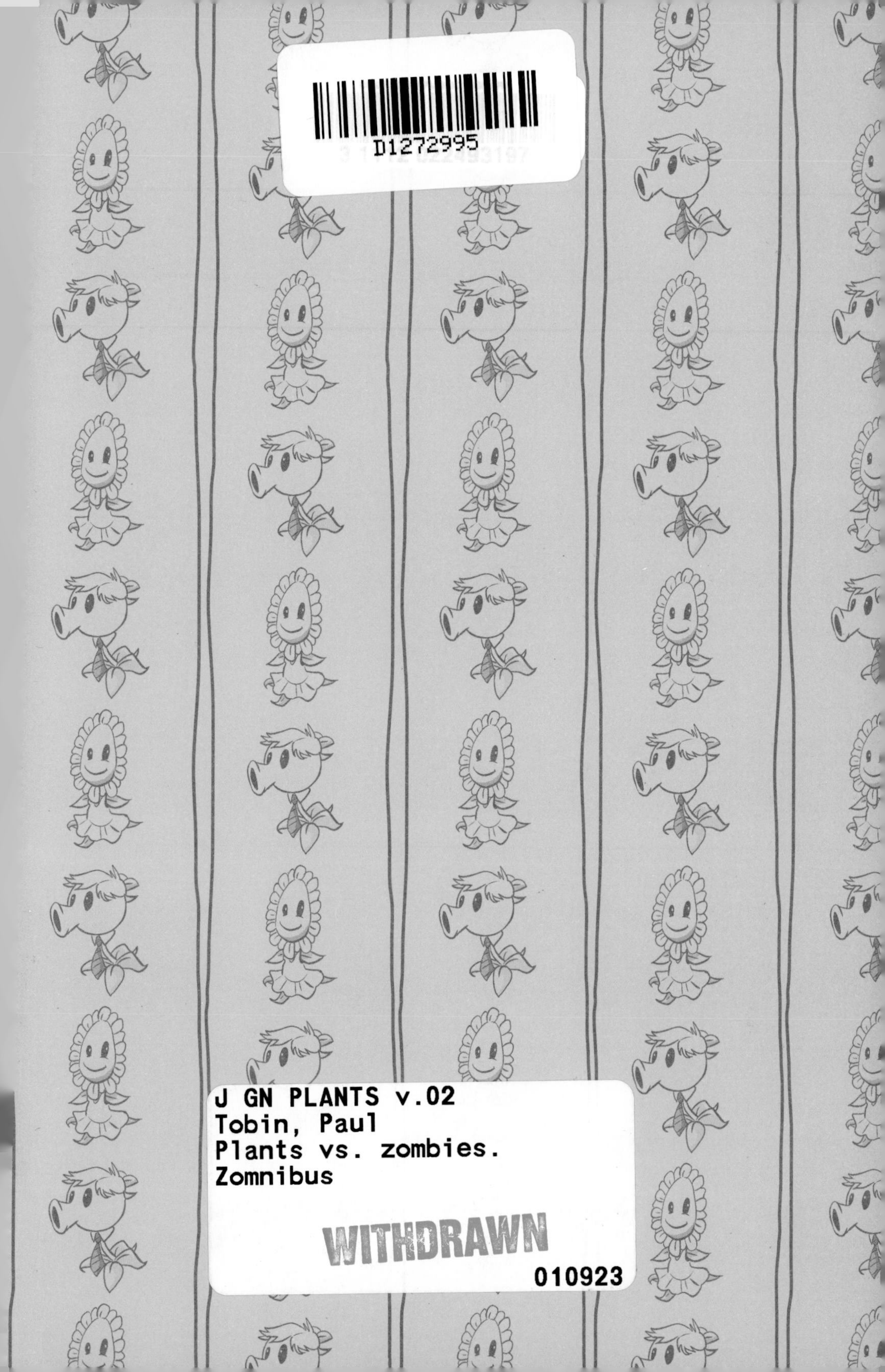

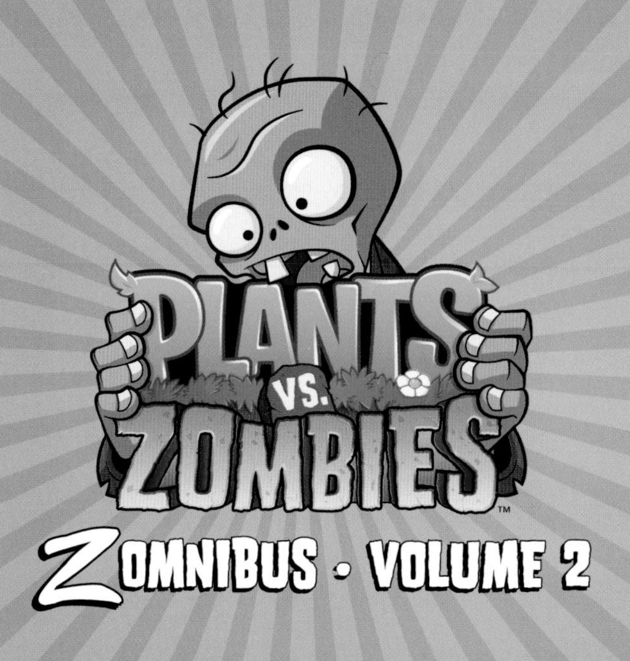
PLANTS VS. ZOMBIES
ZOMNIBUS • VOLUME 2

Written by PAUL TOBIN

Art by ANDIE TONG, RON CHAN, and JACOB CHABOT

Colors by MATT J. RAINWATER

Letters by STEVE DUTRO

Cover by RON CHAN

WITH BONUS STORIES illustrated by Brian Churilla, Karim Friha, Nneka Myers, Cat Farris, Matt J. Rainwater, Rachel Downing, Chris Sheridan, and Jeremy Vanhoozer!

DARK HORSE BOOKS

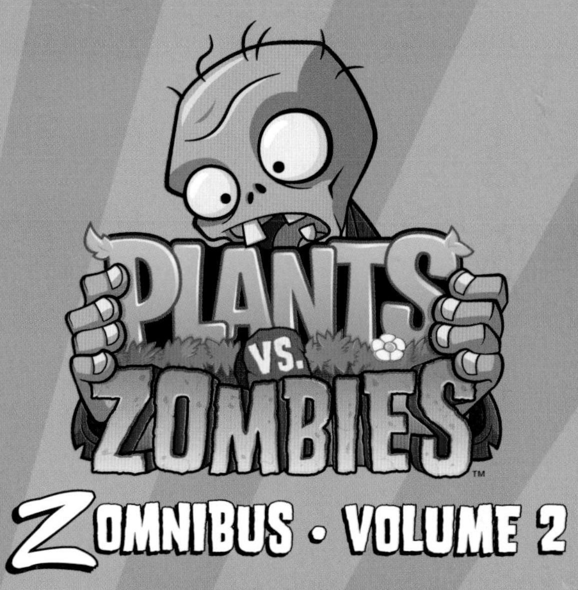
PLANTS VS. ZOMBIES
ZOMNIBUS · VOLUME 2

President and Publisher **MIKE RICHARDSON**
Senior Editor **PHILIP R. SIMON**
Associate Editor **JUDY KHUU**
Assistant Editor **ROSE WEITZ**
Designer **KATHLEEN BARNETT**
Digital Art Technician **ALLYSON HALLER**

Special thanks to Nina Dobner, Joshua Franks, Kristen Star, and everyone at PopCap Games and EA Games.

First Edition: September 2022
Ebook ISBN 978-1-50673-369-2
Hardcover ISBN 978-1-50673-368-5

1 2 3 4 5 6 7 8 9 10
Printed in China

DarkHorse.com
PopCap.com

No plants were harmed in the making of these comics, however, countless zombies, aboveground and belowground, were exhausted by these adventures and needed naps.

This volume collects the Dark Horse comic book series *Plants vs. Zombies* #4-12, including all main and bonus stories found in those comics—also collected as *Plants vs. Zombies: Grown Sweet Home* (comics #4-6), *Plants vs. Zombies: Petal to the Metal* (comics #7-9), and *Plants vs. Zombies: Boom Boom Mushroom* (comics #10-12)—along with the short story "The Lady in Red" from Dark Horse's Free Comic Book Day 2016 comic.

Library of Congress Cataloging-in-Publication Data

Names: Tobin, Paul, 1965- writer. | Chan, Ron, artist | Rainwater, Matthew J., colourist | Dutro, Steve, letterer.
Title: Plants vs. zombies. Zomnibus / writer, Paul Tobin ; artist, Ron Chan ; colors, Matthew J. Rainwater ; letters, Steve Dutro.
Other titles: Plants versus zombies. Zomnibus
Description: First edition. | Milwaukie, OR : Dark Horse Books, 2021- | Series: Plants vs. zombies | v.1: "This volume collects Plants vs. Zombies Volume 1: Lawnmageddon, Volume 2: Timepocalypse, and Volume 3: Bully For You, published November 2013-November 2015."
Identifiers: LCCN 2021014168 (print) | LCCN 2021014169 (ebook) | ISBN 9781506728209 (v. 1 ; hardcover) | ISBN 9781506728216 (v. 1 ; ebook)
Subjects: LCSH: Graphic novels. | CYAC: Graphic novels. | Zombies--Fiction. | Plants--Fiction. | Humorous stories.
Classification: LCC PZ7.7.T62 Prg 2021 (print) | LCC PZ7.7.T62 (ebook) | DDC 741.5/973--dc23
LC record available at https://lccn.loc.gov/2021014168
LC ebook record available at https://lccn.loc.gov/2021014169

TABLE OF CONTENTS

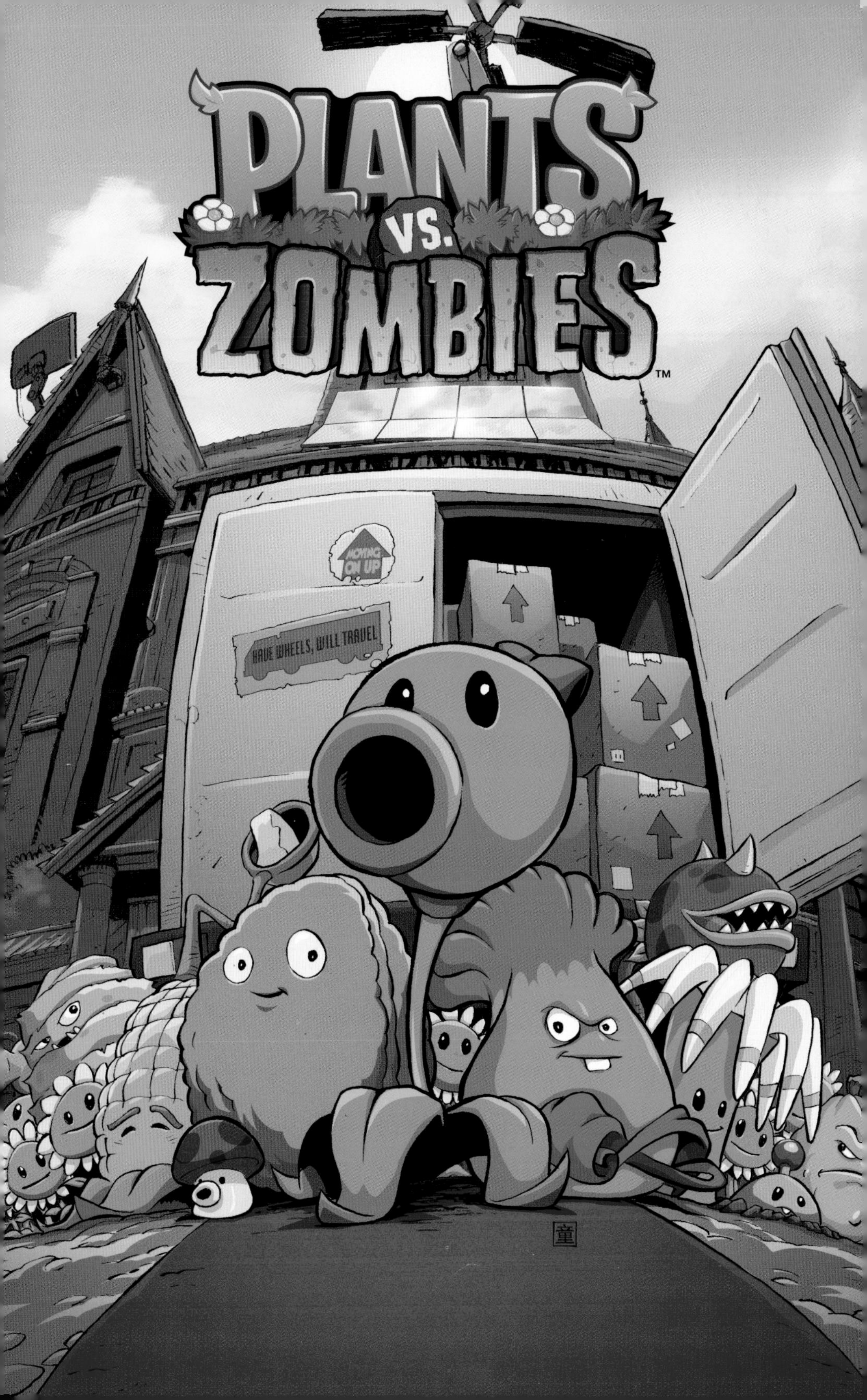
PLANTS VS. ZOMBIES™
MOVING ON UP
HAVE WHEELS, WILL TRAVEL
童

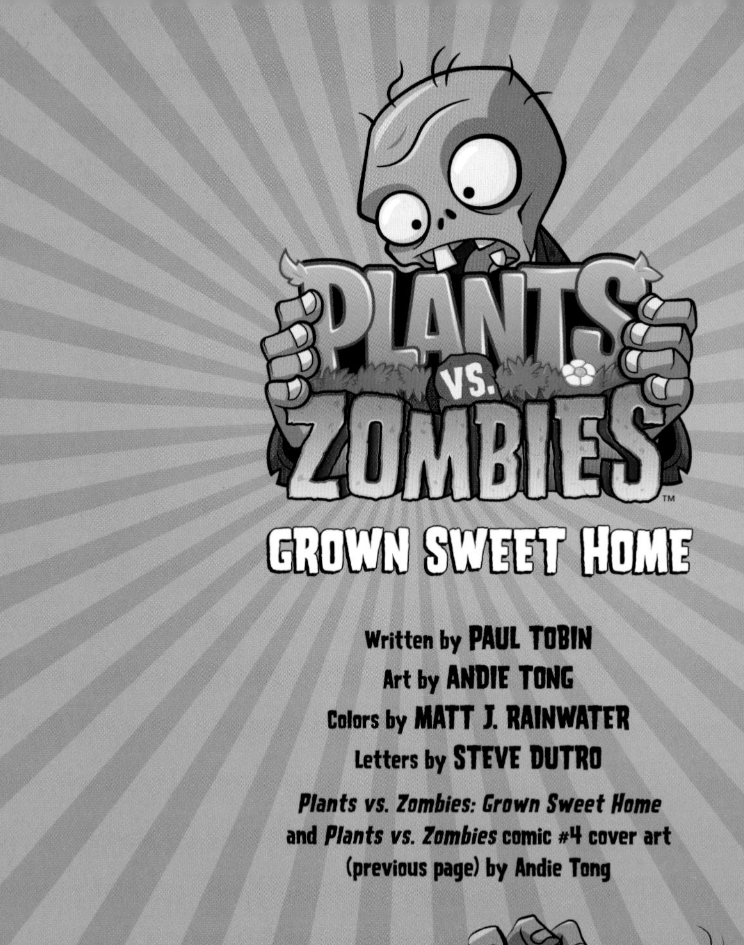

GROWN SWEET HOME

Written by **PAUL TOBIN**
Art by **ANDIE TONG**
Colors by **MATT J. RAINWATER**
Letters by **STEVE DUTRO**

Plants vs. Zombies: Grown Sweet Home and *Plants vs. Zombies* comic #4 cover art (previous page) by Andie Tong

BRAKKA-KA-POWIE!

KRANNG KRANNG

ZINGY-FLOOT!

CRASH!

PEW! PEW!

SMASH!

KABOOOOOOM

UH, IS CRAZY DAVE *STILL* OUT IN HIS GARAGE INVENTING? IT'S, LIKE, *WAAAY* NIGHTTIME.

I KNOW. UNCLE DAVE IS ALWAYS MAKING A RACKET. RIGHT NOW I THINK HE'S WORKING ON...

"...WIND CHIMES!"

BING BING BRONNG BRANG BRANG BRANNG

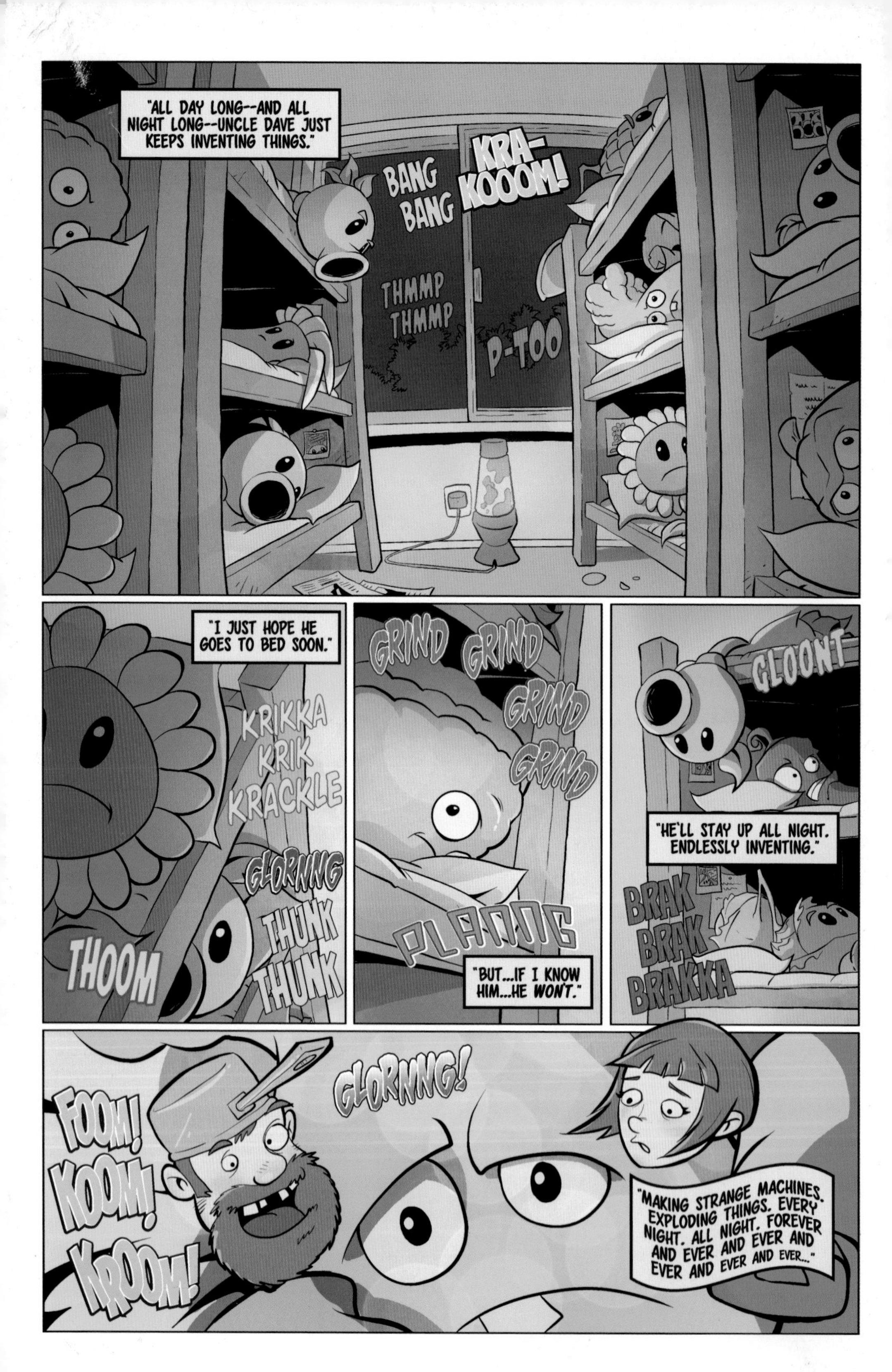
"ALL DAY LONG--AND ALL NIGHT LONG--UNCLE DAVE JUST KEEPS INVENTING THINGS."
BANG BANG
KRA-KOOOM!
THMMP THMMP
P-TOO
"I JUST HOPE HE GOES TO BED SOON."
KRIKKA KRIK KRACKLE
GLORNNG
THUNK THUNK
THOOM
GRIND GRIND GRIND GRIND
PLANNG
"BUT...IF I KNOW HIM...HE *WON'T*."
GLOONT
"HE'LL STAY UP ALL NIGHT. ENDLESSLY INVENTING."
BRAK BRAK BRAKKA
FOOM! KOOM! KROOM!
GLORNNG!
"MAKING STRANGE MACHINES. EXPLODING THINGS. EVERY NIGHT. ALL NIGHT. FOREVER AND EVER AND EVER AND EVER AND EVER AND EVER..."

ONE WEEK LATER...
WOW. THE PLANTS ARE LOOKING... DROOPY. TIRED.
I'M AFRAID IT'S UNCLE DAVE'S FAULT.
GRABFLOOEY! OONK OONK SCROGGLE!
HE INVENTED THIS ROBOT SUN.
"IT KEEPS WANDERING AROUND, WATCHING TELEVISION AT ALL HOURS OF THE NIGHT, CONFUSING THE PLANTS..."
WHRRR
"THEY THINK THE SUN IS UP, AND IT'S TIME TO GET OUT OF BED."
MUNCH MUNCH
WHRRR WHRRR
YAWWWN!
BUT...NO. IT'S JUST THIS MACHINE.
WHRRR WHRRR

THE NEXT DAY...
BANG
BANG
AND THE NEXT...
WHRRR
WHRRR
AND THEN...
HUH?
WHISPER
REALLY?
HONEY B CEREAL
THE PLANTS WANT A PLACE OF THEIR OWN!
UNCLE DAVE, SOME OF THE PLANTS WANT TO MOVE OUT. TO BE INDEPENDENT.
FRED THE SUNFLOWER, JEFF THE BLOOMERANG, AND GRRAWRR-BEAR THE ULTIMATE FACE PUNCHER... THEY TALKED TO SOME OF THE OTHERS, AND A GROUP OF THEM THINK IT'S TIME.

BUT ARE THEY OLD ENOUGH TO GET A PLACE OF THEIR OWN? CAN THEY REALLY TAKE CARE OF THEMSELVES?
WHAT IF THEY GET INTO TROUBLE?
HMMM...
HMMM...
I SUPPOSE WE'LL HAVE TO ASK CRAZY DAVE.
YEAH. UNCLE DAVE, WOULD IT BE OKAY IF SOME OF THE PLANTS GOT A HOUSE OF THEIR OWN?
WE COULD LET THEM USE THE OLD MANSION.
TAP
TAP
TAP
HRN?
SNORE!
DROOL
SNOOOOORE!
I THINK HE'S OKAY WITH IT.

AND SO...
UNCLE DAVE SAYS HE'S HAD THE HEAT, ELECTRICITY, AND WATER ALL HOOKED UP--AS WELL AS THE MORE IMPORTANT UTILITIES, LIKE ICE CREAM AND TOAST.
YOU PLANTS CAN HAVE YOUR OWN ROOMS. THERE'S, LIKE... HUNDREDS.
POP!
GAH!
AND HERE'S A PHONE, SO YOU CALL US IF YOU NEED ANYTHING. AND DON'T WORRY--WE'LL VISIT EVERY DAY.
NOW, GOODBYE, TAKE CARE, AND DON'T FORGET TO BRUSH YOUR TEETH... IF YOU HAVE THEM.

DAY-ONE VISIT.
GUYS, YOU CAN'T ALWAYS HAVE THE TUB. JEFF'S GETTING ALL GRUBBY.
THOONT
P-TANG
THOONT THOONT
PANNG
DAY-TWO VISIT.
THE HALLWAYS ARE NOT THE PROPER PLACE FOR A SHOOTING GALLERY!
DAY-THREE VISIT.
GUYS. SERIOUSLY, IT'S JUST A SLOGAN. SUNLIGHT PIZZA DOESN'T REALLY HAVE "SUNLIGHT IN EVERY SLICE," NO MATTER HOW MANY... UMM...THOUSANDS OF DOLLARS OF PIZZA YOU ORDER.
EXPLAIN TO ME AGAIN HOW THIS HAPPENED?
DAY-FOUR VISIT.

SO...FINALLY...
OKAY. YOU GUYS OBVIOUSLY NEED SOME GUIDANCE IN LIFE AND SOME HELPFUL HINTS ON HOW TO LIVE ON YOUR OWN, SO WE'RE ALL GOING TO HELP YOU.
HERE'S HOW YOU DO LAUNDRY.
AND HERE'S HOW TO MAKE A SIMPLE, COST-EFFECTIVE MEAL FOR THE ENTIRE HOUSE.
OCCASIONALLY, HOME REPAIRS ARE NEEDED.
LET'S SEE HOW MUCH YOU CAN LEARN WHILE WE REMODEL THIS PORCH INTO A SUNROOM.
IT'S IMPORTANT TO GET ALONG WITH YOUR ROOMMATES.
PLANNING DAILY EVENTS TOGETHER CAN BRING US ALL CLOSER.

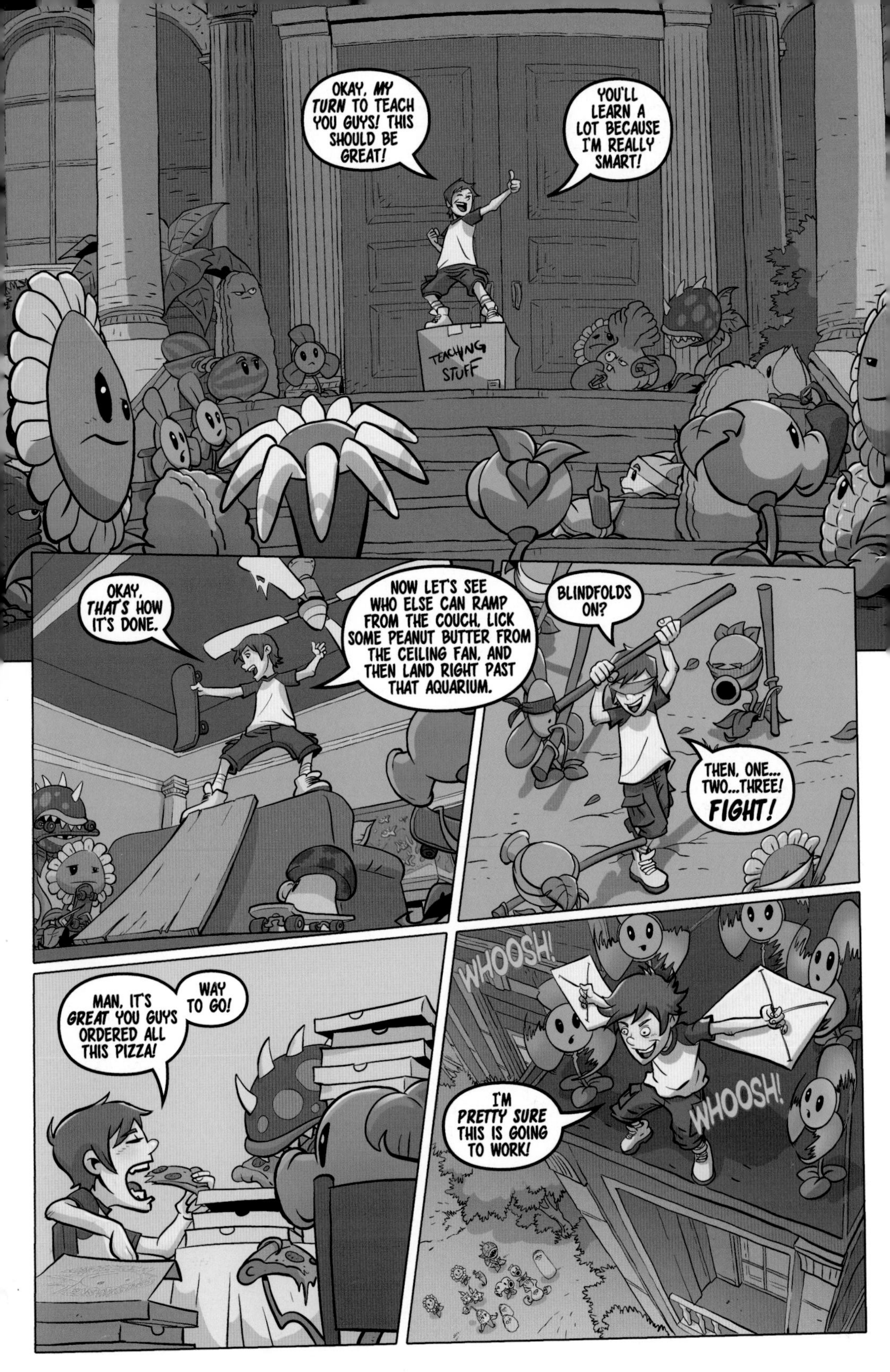
OKAY, MY TURN TO TEACH YOU GUYS! THIS SHOULD BE GREAT!
YOU'LL LEARN A LOT BECAUSE I'M REALLY SMART!
TEACHING STUFF
OKAY, THAT'S HOW IT'S DONE.
NOW LET'S SEE WHO ELSE CAN RAMP FROM THE COUCH, LICK SOME PEANUT BUTTER FROM THE CEILING FAN, AND THEN LAND RIGHT PAST THAT AQUARIUM.
BLINDFOLDS ON?
THEN, ONE... TWO...THREE! FIGHT!
MAN, IT'S GREAT YOU GUYS ORDERED ALL THIS PIZZA!
WAY TO GO!
WHOOSH!
I'M PRETTY SURE THIS IS GOING TO WORK!
WHOOSH!

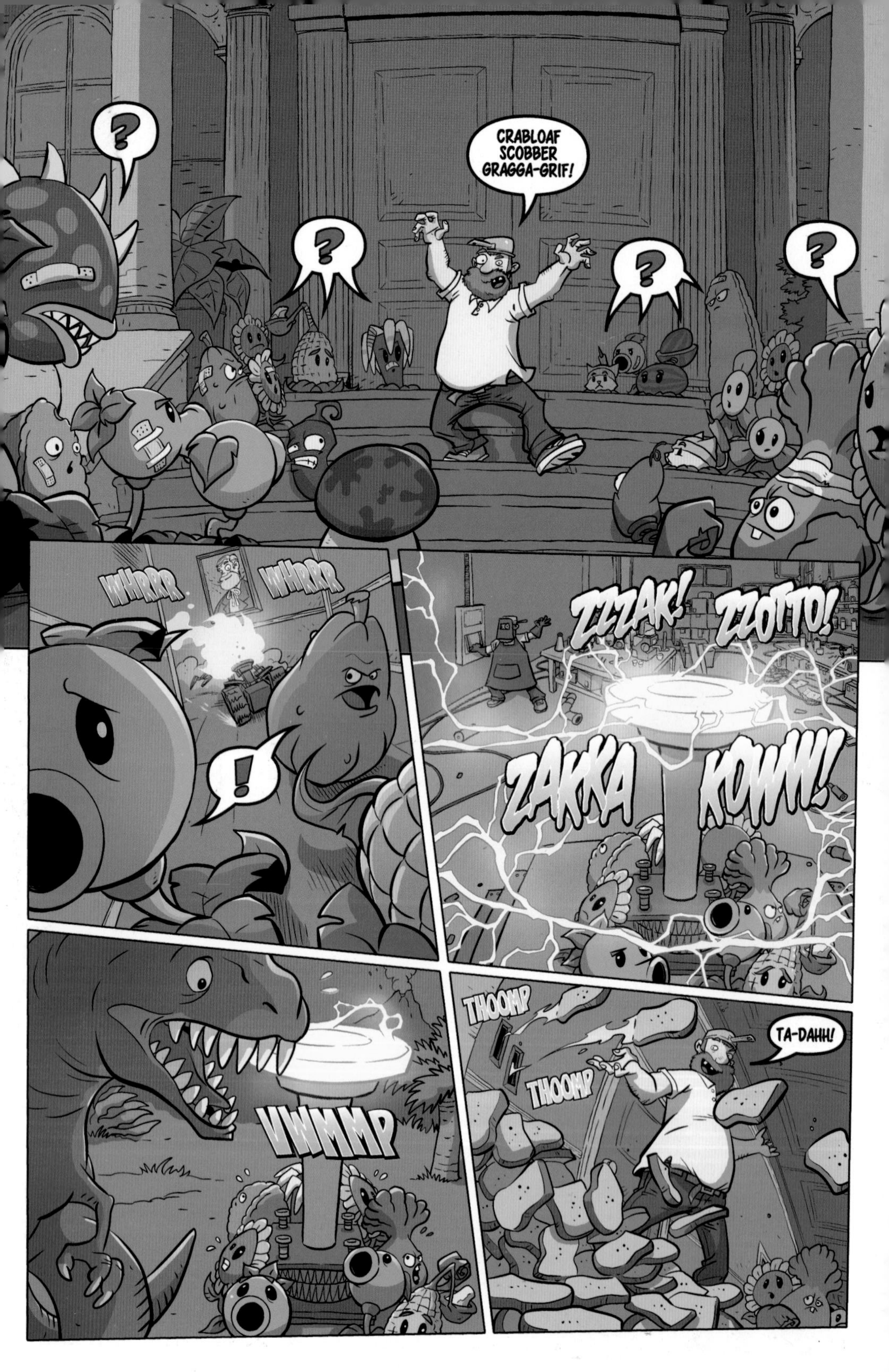
?
CRABLOAF SCOBBER GRAGGA-GRIF!
?
?
?
WHRRR
WHRRR
!
ZZZAK!
ZZOTTO!
ZAKKA
KOWW!
VWMMP
THOOMP
THOOMP
TA-DAHH!

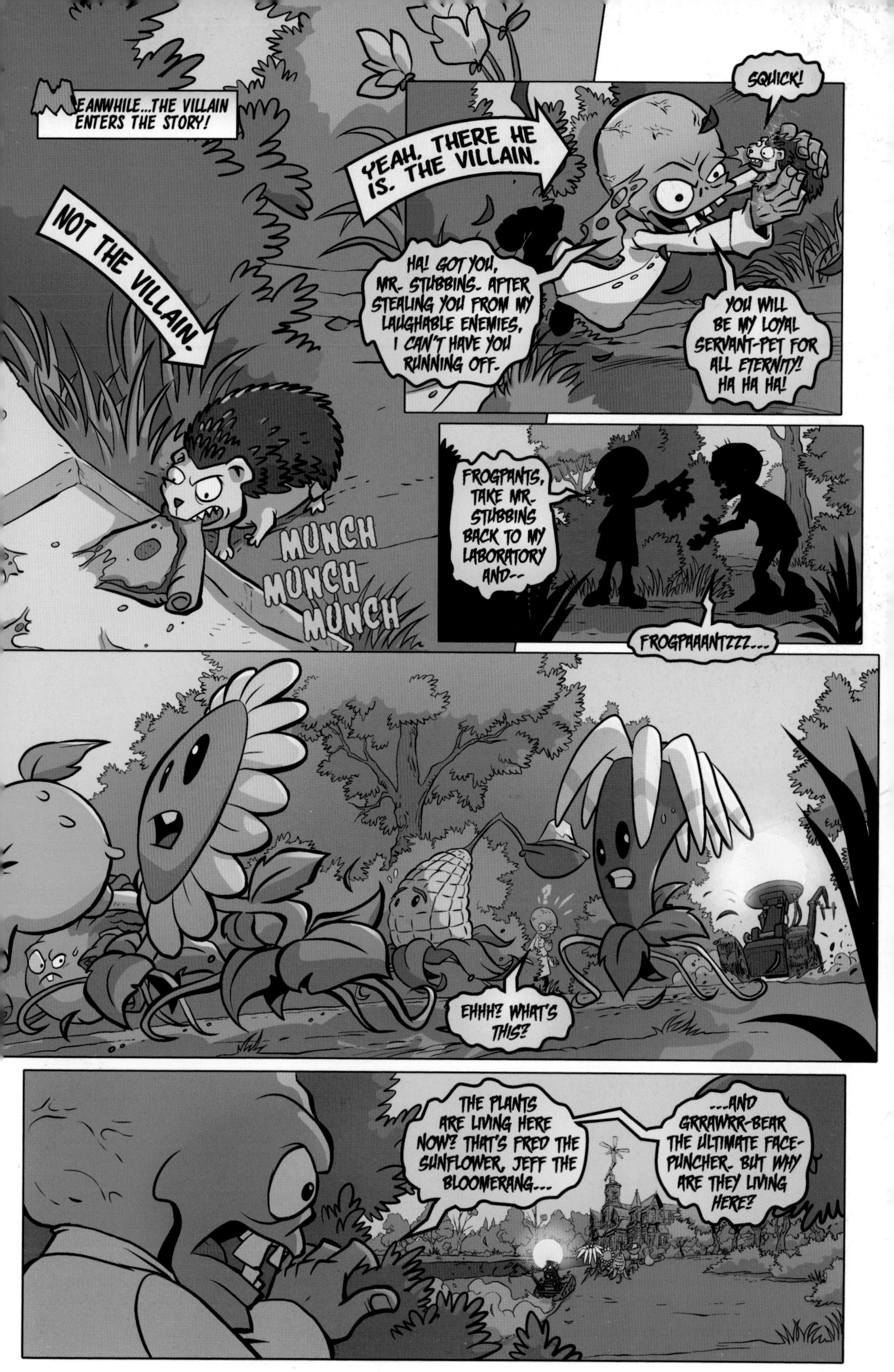
MEANWHILE...THE VILLAIN ENTERS THE STORY!
NOT THE VILLAIN.
YEAH, THERE HE IS. THE VILLAIN.
SQUICK!
HA! GOT YOU, MR. STUBBINS. AFTER STEALING YOU FROM MY LAUGHABLE ENEMIES, I CAN'T HAVE YOU RUNNING OFF.
YOU WILL BE MY LOYAL SERVANT-PET FOR ALL ETERNITY! HA HA HA!
MUNCH
MUNCH
MUNCH
FROGPANTS, TAKE MR. STUBBING BACK TO MY LABORATORY AND--
FROGPAAANTZZZ...
EHHH? WHAT'S THIS?
THE PLANTS ARE LIVING HERE NOW? THAT'S FRED THE SUNFLOWER, JEFF THE BLOOMERANG...
...AND GRRAWRR-BEAR THE ULTIMATE FACE-PUNCHER. BUT WHY ARE THEY LIVING HERE?

GUYS, IT'S IMPORTANT THAT YOU UNDERSTAND WHAT WE'RE TELLING YOU.
WELL, IT'S NOT QUITE AS IMPORTANT TO LISTEN TO WHAT *NATE* TELLS YOU.
OR *UNCLE DAVE*, FOR THAT MATTER-- UNLESS HE'S TEACHING YOU ABOUT ICE CREAM, BECAUSE *THEN* YOU SHOULD LISTEN.

THE THING IS, YOU NEED TO *LISTEN*... TO LEARN HOW TO BE SELF-SUFFICIENT AND HOW TO FIT INTO HUMAN SOCIETY.
Z

AND THEN NOBODY WILL EVEN KNOW THE DIFFERENCE BETWEEN YOU AND ANYBODY ELSE.

AHHH!
AHHH!
AHHH!
AHHH!
HMMM... SOUNDS LIKE VALUABLE LESSONS INDEED. WHILE I MYSELF CAN SEAMLESSLY FIT IN WITH HUMAN SOCIETY WITHOUT ANYONE KNOWING THE DIFFERENCE...
AHHH!
AHHH!
AHHH!
BRAINS?
...MY ARMY CANNOT.
NO ZOMBEZ IN HERE!
DISGUIZ
SHUFFLE SHUFFLE SHUFFLE
"THERE'S ONLY ONE THING TO DO. FIRST...AIMING AT THE MANSION'S WEAKEST LINK, I WILL ENACT A SERIES OF CLEVER RUSES TO GAIN ACCESS TO THE HOUSE."
DING DONNNG!
SOMEONE'S AT THE DOOR!
UNSUZPISHIOUS CABLE GUYZ
HUH? "CABLE GUYS"...?

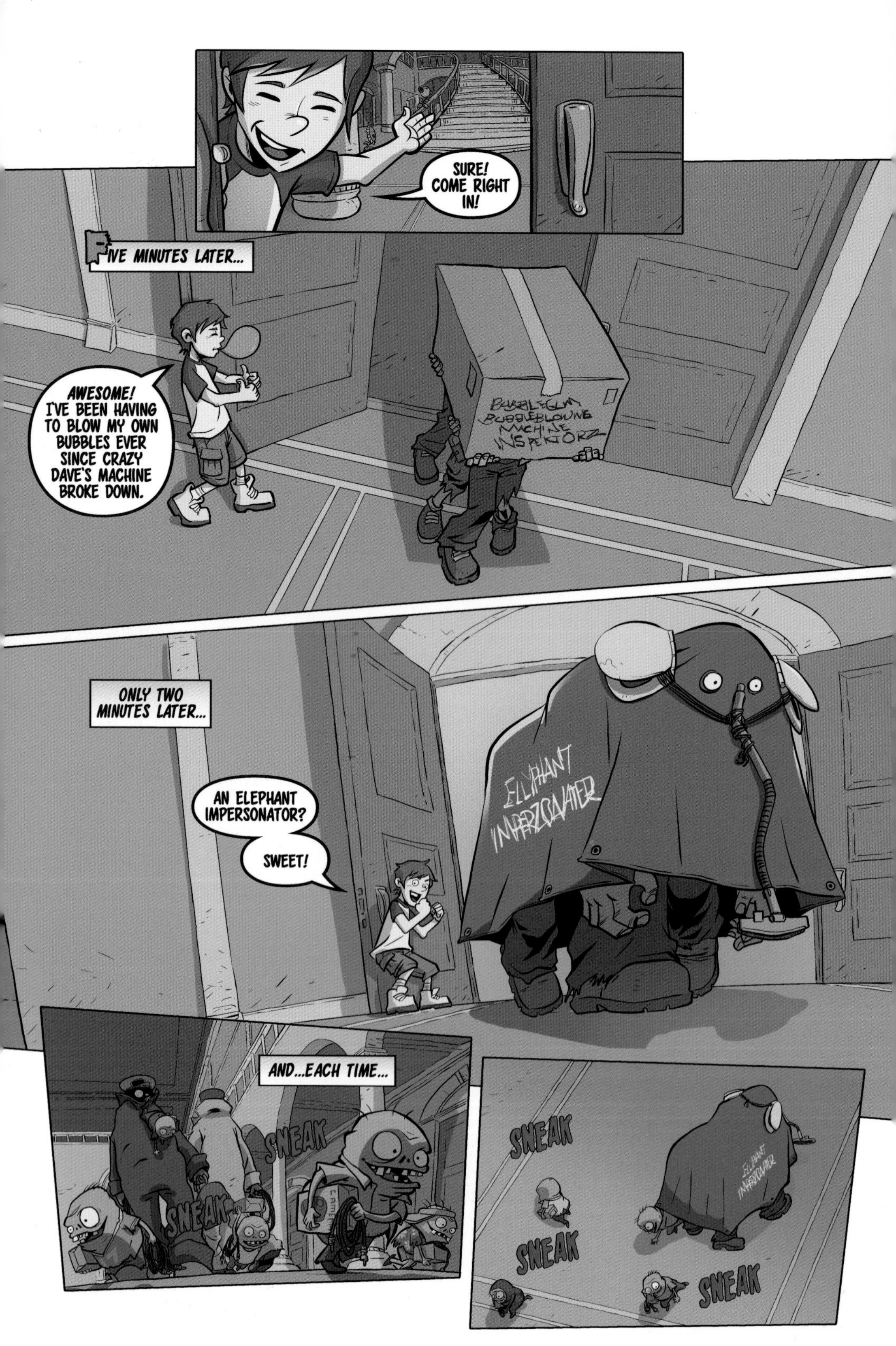
SURE! COME RIGHT IN!
FIVE MINUTES LATER...
AWESOME! I'VE BEEN HAVING TO BLOW MY OWN BUBBLES EVER SINCE CRAZY DAVE'S MACHINE BROKE DOWN.
BUBBLEGUM BUBBLEBLOWING MACHINE INSPEKTORZ
ONLY TWO MINUTES LATER...
AN ELEPHANT IMPERSONATOR?
SWEET!
AND...EACH TIME...
SNEAK
SNEAK
SNEAK
SNEAK
SNEAK

INSTALL
SNEAK
"AND NOW---THE SECOND PART OF MY PLAN!"
INSTALL INSTALL
THUMP
THEN, FINALLY...
HA! MY CAMERAS HAVE BEEN SECRETLY INSTALLED ALL OVER THE HOUSE!
NOW I WILL LEARN EVERYTHING THAT THOSE INFURIATING PLANTS ARE LEARNING.
THE SECRETS OF ACTING HUMAN WILL BE MINE! MINE!
WHAT ARE YOU DOING?
THOSE POP SMART SNACKS ARE MINE! MINE!
SWAT!

AND SO...
OKAY, EVERYONE... REMEMBER HOW TO FOLD YOUR LAUNDRY?

MEANWHILE...
ARRGH! PUT A CREASE IN THE SLEEVE! SHE SAID TO PUT A CREASE IN THE SLEEVE!
MUNCH
MUNCH
MUNCH

FOR DISHWASHING, PUT A LITTLE DISHWASHING LIQUID ON THE SPONGE.

MEANWHILE...
BRAAAINS.
FLURRT

VACUUM REGULARLY-- TO KEEP YOUR HOUSE CLEAN.
VRRRRRRRR

HA! I INVENTED A MUCH BIGGER VACUUM, IN ORDER TO SPEED UP THE PROCESS.
I WIN THIS ONE, HUMANS!
WHRRRRRRRR
RRRRR

FLOPPLE VANHOOZER HORGPORK!
DAVE SAYS TO ADJUST THE SEAT, CHECK THE MIRRORS, AND THEN START THE CAR.

NOW JUST ACCELERATE SMOOTHLY. GOOD...NICE AND EASY.

AND NOW... JUST ACCELERATE SMOOTHLY.

ONE SECOND LATER...
VROOOM
GAH! HOW IS THIS POSSIBLE?

AND ALSO...
YOU WALK UP, SMILE, AND SHAKE HANDS.

MEANWHILE...
GOOD. EVEN BETTER THAN THE PLANTS DID!
BRAINS!
BRAINS!
BRAINS!
BRAINS!
BRAINS!
BRAINS!!
BRAINS!

SOON...
HMMM. MY ZOMBIES ARE MAKING GOOD PROGRESS THANKS TO THESE SECRET LESSONS, BUT...
"...I NEED ANSWERS THAT THOSE PLANTS AREN'T ASKING. TIME FOR A CLEVER PLAN TO REVEAL THE REAL SECRETS TO ACTING HUMAN."
SHFF!
POP!
HUH? A LETTER?
POP!
BLOWING MACHINE
IT'S FROM PATRICE!
NOT-SUSPICIOUS LETTER FOR NATE THE HUMAN BOY. FROM PATRICE THE HUMAN GIRL.
THINGS TO BE TEACHING THE ~~WRETCHED~~ ~~STUPID~~ NICE PLANTS.
1: HOW DOES HUMANS EAT BRAINS?
2: SECRETS OF NEIGHBORVILLE'S WEAK POINTS?
3: HOW TO MAKE DOGS NOT BITE AND BARK?
4: ARE SELFIES REALLY SO BAD?
5: WALKING FASTER THAN A WAFFLE: HOW IS IT DONE?

THIS HANDWRITING. SOMETHING'S WEIRD ABOUT IT.
BRAINS?
UH-OH. HAS HE UNCOVERED MY SCHEME?
BUT MY PLAN WAS FLAWLESS!
EH?
I MEAN, PATRICE'S HANDWRITING IS HORRIBLE!
MY HANDWRITING IS MUCH BETTER!
HMPH.
NATE'S TO-DO LIST
1. EAT PIZZA
2. ARMPIT FART CHAMPIONSHIPS
3. CHECK TO MAKE SURE I ATE PIZZA

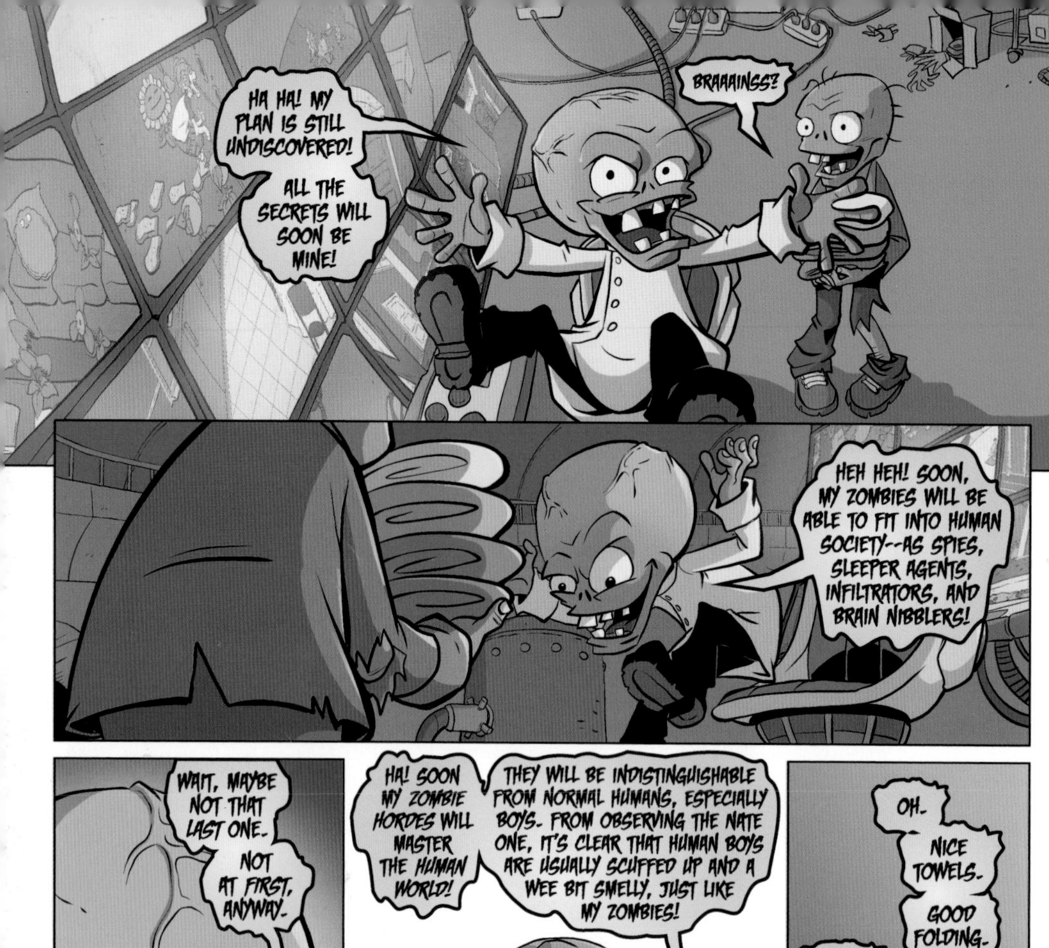
HA HA! MY PLAN IS STILL UNDISCOVERED!
ALL THE SECRETS WILL SOON BE MINE!
BRAAAINSS?
HEH HEH! SOON, MY ZOMBIES WILL BE ABLE TO FIT INTO HUMAN SOCIETY--AS SPIES, SLEEPER AGENTS, INFILTRATORS, AND BRAIN NIBBLERS!

WAIT, MAYBE NOT THAT LAST ONE.
NOT AT FIRST, ANYWAY.
RUB RUB
HA! SOON MY ZOMBIE HORDES WILL MASTER THE HUMAN WORLD!
THEY WILL BE INDISTINGUISHABLE FROM NORMAL HUMANS, ESPECIALLY BOYS. FROM OBSERVING THE NATE ONE, IT'S CLEAR THAT HUMAN BOYS ARE USUALLY SCUFFED UP AND A WEE BIT SMELLY, JUST LIKE MY ZOMBIES!
HA HA HEH HEH!
HA HA HA HA!

OH.
NICE TOWELS.
GOOD FOLDING.
BRAINS!

HOW IS THIS EVEN POSSIBLE?
SPLURGLE

WRONG.
RRRRRRRRR
CHOPPA CHOPPY
RRRRRR

NOPE.

LISTEN UP, EVERYONE! OUR MENTORSHIP PROGRAM OBVIOUSLY NEEDS A LITTLE MORE INCENTIVE. SO, STARTING TODAY...
...WE'LL BE GIVING REWARDS TO THE PLANTS THAT DO THE BEST JOB! REWARDS LIKE...

COMIC BOOKS!
CANDY BARS!
AND THE GRAND PRIZE... A NEW BIKE!

MADE THE BED! REWARD-- TWO CANDY BARS!
DOOMCHEW!
DISHES DONE! REWARD-- SERGEANT SUSPENDERS #1!
HOMEMADE SPARKLING PEPPERONI PIZZA WITH CRÈME BRÛLÉE DESSERT! REWARD-- TWO GOLD STARS!
YEP!
NOPE!
LAUNDRY FINISHED! REWARD-- THREE CANDY BARS!
NOTHING'S ON FIRE! GRAND PRIZE! NEW BIKE!

MEANWHILE...
HMMM...
SO, AFTER WATCHING THE PAST FEW DAYS THROUGH MY EXTENSIVE NETWORK OF HIDDEN CAMERAS, I HAVE COME TO TWO CONCLUSIONS!
"FIRST, NATHAN TIMELY SNEAKS COLD PIZZA FROM THE REFRIGERATOR EVERY NIGHT."
AND, SECOND... APPARENTLY, BEING NICE TO PEOPLE AND GIVING THEM REWARDS IS ACTUALLY AN INCENTIVE TO DO A BETTER JOB.
NOW SERVING NUMBER 1348
PUNISHMENT ROOM
HMMM...
HM.
HMMM...
SO BE IT!
I SHALL TRY THIS BOLD NEW PLAN!

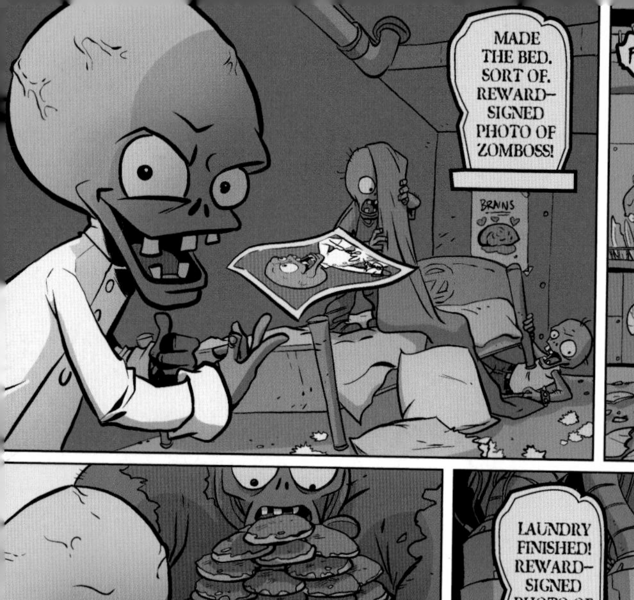
MADE THE BED. SORT OF. REWARD— SIGNED PHOTO OF ZOMBOSS!
BRAINS

FROGPAAAANTS...
FINISHED THE DISHES WITH LESS THAN HALF BROKEN! REWARD— SIGNED PHOTO OF ZOMBOSS!

PROPERLY PREPARED POP SMARTS DISH (STRAWBERRY, GRAPE, AND ISAAC NEWTON FLAVORS). REWARD— SIGNED PHOTO OF ZOMBOSS!

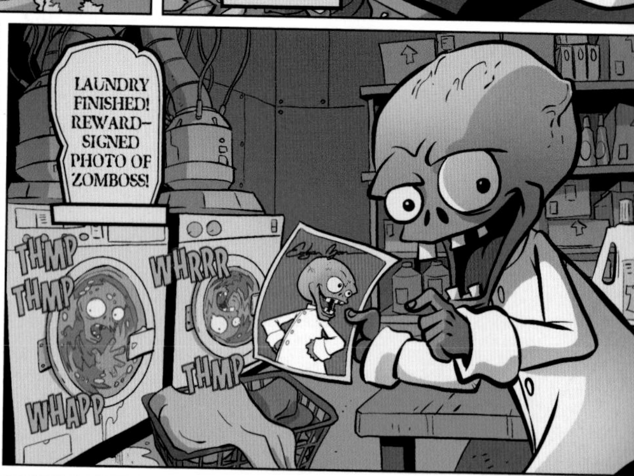
LAUNDRY FINISHED! REWARD— SIGNED PHOTO OF ZOMBOSS!
THMP
THMP
WHRRR
THMP
WHAPP

NiGeL
NOTHING MUCH ON FIRE! GRAND PRIZE! EXTRA-LARGE SIGNED PHOTO OF ZOMBOSS!

OKAY, EVERYONE, WE'RE GOING TO TRY A FEW SIMPLE TASKS.
AND, FIRST... I WANT YOU TO KNOW THAT I HAVE THE UTMOST FAITH IN YOU.
NIGEL
DO NOT FAIL ME, YOU MINDLESS FOOLS.
OKAY, LET'S ALL LEARN HOW TO TIE SOME SHOELACES. OUT IN THE REAL WORLD, THIS IS ALMOST AS IMPORTANT AS PIZZA EATING!
BUT...NO PRESSURE. IT'S JUST IMPORTANT THAT YOU TRY.
AND IF THESE CRETINS FAIL TO PROPERLY TIE THE SHOELACES, THEN... YOU STRIKE!
LET ME SHOW YOU THE RIGHT WAY TO OPEN A CAN OF SOUP.
FIRST, IT'S IMPORTANT TO USE THE PROPER TOOLS.
STRIKE!

HERE'S A VERY IMPORTANT SKILL.
IT'S CALLED... "TEXTING FART JOKES TO YOUR FRIENDS."
2. CLICK
4. CLICK
SEND
5. HAHAHAHAHA!
MUNCH
MUNCH
BRAINS?
BRAINS?
BRAINS?
GIVE THAT... BACK!
MUNCH
ORDERING PIZZA!
EEEAAAAAEEEAAAAAHH!
WATCHING TELEVISION!
WE NOW RETURN TO...THE LAST HOUSE ON THE LEAF.
AND NOW, HOUR THIRTY-FIVE OF THE ZOMBOSS LECTURES.
OOOH, ONE OF MY FAVORITES!
AND... MORE POPCORN, LACKWIT!

CLEANING YOUR HOUSE IS AN IMPORTANT PART OF LIVING ALONE. LET'S LEARN BY VACUUMING THIS CARPETING.
VVVOOOOMMM
HOW DID THIS HAPPEN?
BRAINS?
BRAINS?
VVVBLURK GLURK VVVOOOOMMM
LET'S LEARN HOW TO MOW THE LAWN!
RRRWWWWWRRRRR
OOOH! THAT...DID NOT GO WELL.
RRRWWWRRR
CHNNK CHNNK
CHOPPY
RRWWWRR
SEWING PRACTICE!
BRAINS?
BRAINS?
AND THIS IS HOW YOU SEW YOUR SHIRT BACK TOGETHER AFTER A MOWING ACCIDENT.

WELL, EVERYONE, I THINK YOU'VE LEARNED ABOUT ALL YOU CAN FROM BOOKS.
BUT BOOK LEARNING AND CLASSROOM LEARNING ONLY GO SO FAR.
WHAT YOU NEED IS REAL-WORLD EXPERIENCE.
SO, IN ORDER FOR YOU TO LEARN AND FIT INTO SOCIETY, WE'RE GOING TO STEP THINGS UP.
BASICALLY, WE'RE GOING TO THROW YOU INTO THE DEEP END OF THE POOL.
THAT'S JUST A METAPHOR, OF COURSE. WE WOULDN'T BE STUPID ENOUGH TO REALLY THROW YOU INTO A POOL.
SAY WHAT?
TOSS!
BLRR... BLRGG... BRAINS?

LATER, ON THE STREETS OF NEIGHBORVILLE...
COME ON!
WAVE WAVE
POINT
DISGUISES!
?
YOU'RE DOING GREAT, EVERYONE!
sniff
sniff

WHILE ELSEWHERE...
COACH
COME ON...
WAVE
WAVE
WAVE
DISGUISES!
COLOGNE!
COLOGNE!
COLOGNE!
MASK!
AH, MY BRILLIANT PLAN IS WORKING! NOBODY SUSPECTS A THING.
WHAT IS UP? or DOWN?
HOW ARE YOU TODAY? I AM QUITE FINE AND VERY HUMAN!
HELLO FELLOW HUMANS
HOW IS THE WEATHER?

MEANWHILE...
OKAY, JUST ACT NORMAL.
LIKE... HUMAN NORMAL.
00:02
YOUNG LADY? I HAVE TO PAY THE PARKING METER.
COULD YOU HOLD MY MR. GUM-GUMS FOR A BIT?
YOU'VE DONE WELL, YOUNG GIRL! I THINK YOU AND YOUR FRIENDS HAVE ALL EARNED SHINY NICKELS!
HERE'S ONE FOR YOU...
...AND YOU...
...AND YOU...
...AND YOU...

AND YOU...
BARK
BARK
BARK
BARK
DUNN DUNN DUNNNN
DUNN DUNN DUNNNN
LEO, TURN YOUR MUSIC DOWN!
DUNN DUNN DUNNNN
NIGEL

OKAY, EVERYONE, THIS IS...AN UNEXPECTED TEST, BUT...
...JUST REMEMBER YOUR TRAINING...
...AND KEEP CALM...
...AND SIMPLY INTERACT LIKE A HUMAN WOULD DO...
...AND THAT WOULD MAKE ME PROUD.
...AND THEN I WON'T HAVE TO DESTROY YOU.

YOU CAN DO IT. JUST ACT... HUMAN.
POOK POOK POOK WHP WHP WHP PHOOT PHOOT PHOOT
ARE THEY... RUNNING IN FEAR?
YES! IT'S FANTASTIC! DON'T YOU SEE? IT'S WHAT A NORMAL HUMAN WOULD DO! OUR TRAINING IS WORKING!

HMM, THEY THINK THEY CAN DEFEAT US AT THE RUSE OF BEING HUMAN, DO THEY? WELL, THE FORCES OF ZOMBOSS ARE IN-DEFEATABLE!
OR---UN-DEFEATABLE!
ANTI-DEFEATABLE?
ARGH! WHATEVER THE WORD IS!
NIGEL
BRAINS?
DO HUMAN THINGS!
HMM, WAIT- WHAT EXACTLY DO HUMANS DO? I GUESS THEY--- DON'T EAT BRAINS?
YES! THAT'S IT! NOBODY EAT ANY BRAINS!
?!?
NIGEL
BRAINS?
BRAINS?
BRAINS?
BRAINS?
BRAINS?
MEANWHILE...
BOIL
BLURGLE
BOIL

BARGAL BLEC. SPAG SPAG SPAG BRIFFLE?
IT'S UNCLE DAVE. HE'S CALLING FOR ADVICE ON HOW TO MAKE SPAGHETTI.
HE OFTEN HAS...TROUBLE WITH THAT.
IT'S REALLY EASY, UNCLE DAVE.
JUST WATER AND SPAGHETTI AND YOU BOIL IT.
HRM...
ELSE.
UNCLE DAVE JUST ACCIDENTALLY INVENTED ANTIGRAVITY GOLDFISH.
WHAT? BUT...?
I DON'T EVEN...
SERIOUSLY, HOW DOES HE DO THESE THINGS?
OH?
GORFLIPPLE CARASSIUS. AURATUS AURATUS SLAMBANG?

NOT IMPORTANT. WHAT'S IMPORTANT IS THAT WE CAN'T KEEP RUNNING.
TELL ME ABOUT IT!
huff! puff! puff! huff!
WHAT I MEAN IS--WE CAN'T LET THE ZOMBIES HAVE THE RUN OF THIS TOWN!
WE HAVE TO DEFEAT THEM!
YAY. DEFEAT.
huff! puff! puff!
I AM BETTER THAN YOU AT ANYTHING--INCLUDING BEING A HUMAN!
!!
HA! WILL ME!
I MEAN, LOOK AT THOSE PLANTS! SO POORLY DISGUISED!
THERE'S ONLY ONE WAY TO SETTLE WHO'S BETTER, SO...

HI FELLOE HUMANZ
LET THE PLANNNTS VERSUS ZOMMMBIES "ACT LIKE A HUMAN" BATTLE BEGIN!

FIRST CONTEST! HAIRCUTS!
NATE... NO.
ZOMBIES WIN!
RRRRRRRRR CHOPPY-CHOP RRRRRRRRRRR SHKK! SHKK! SHKK! RRRRRRRR
SECOND CONTEST! HOMEWORK!
THE SQUARE ROOT OF 200 = 10 * (2)^(1/2).
THE FIRST KNOWN USE OF THE WORD "PIZZA" WAS IN THE ITALIAN CITY OF GAETA IN THE YEAR 997...
...BUT THE WORD DIDN'T REACH AMERICA UNTIL THE YEAR 1904, WHEN IT WAS PRINTED IN A BOSTON JOURNAL ARTICLE.
RRR! HRRR!
DOES ANYONE HAVE HOMEWORK? DOES ANYONE KNOW WHAT HOMEWORK IS?
CHEW CHOMP
MUNCH
PLANTS WIN!

WALK THE DOGS!
SKIP!
SKIP!
TROT!
TROT!
TROT!

SLINK!
SLINK!
SHIVER
A TIE, I GUESS?!?

CLANG
CLANG
CLANG
TWEEEET
FIVE O'CLOCK!
WOOOOO!
AWOOO!
RING
RING
RING

OH! HEAR THAT?
YES. IT'S FIVE O'CLOCK, AND IN HUMAN TERMS, THAT MEANS...
...IT'S TIME TO QUIT WORK FOR THE DAY...
...AND GO HOME!
NIGEL
HRN?

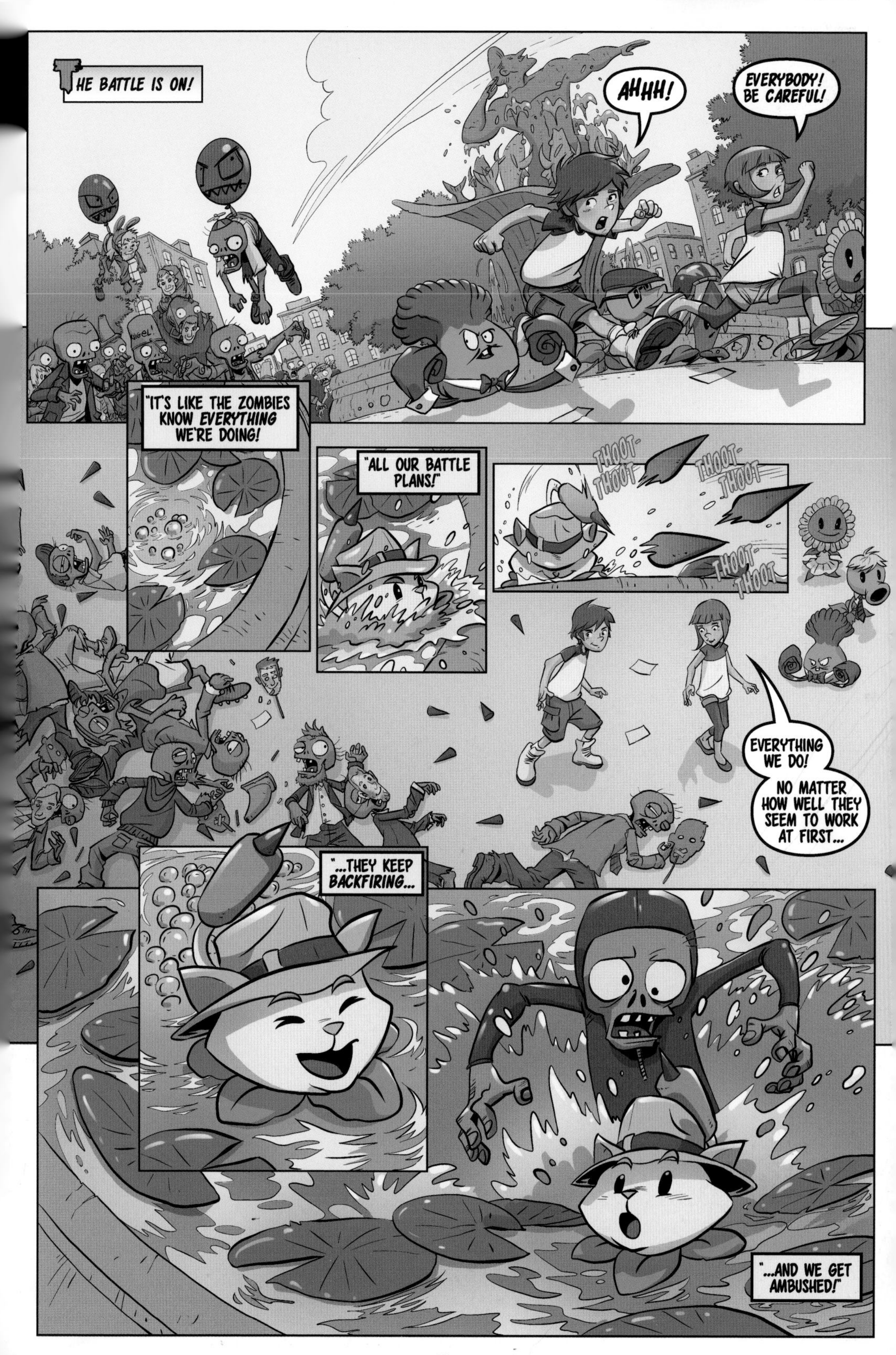
THE BATTLE IS ON!
AHHH!
EVERYBODY! BE CAREFUL!
NIGEL
"IT'S LIKE THE ZOMBIES KNOW EVERYTHING WE'RE DOING!
"ALL OUR BATTLE PLANS!"
THOOT-THOOT
THOOT-THOOT
THOOT-THOOT
EVERYTHING WE DO!
NO MATTER HOW WELL THEY SEEM TO WORK AT FIRST...
"...THEY KEEP BACKFIRING...
"...AND WE GET AMBUSHED!"

FALL BACK! FALL BACK! THE ZOMBIES ARE OVERWHELMING US!
HOW CAN THIS BE? HOW DO THE ZOMBIES KEEP GETTING THE JUMP ON US?
GRAB!
"AFTER ALL...YOU AND I SPENT ALL NIGHT PLANNING OUR STRATEGIES!"
GLARE!
UH, OKAY, WHAT I MEANT IS...
"...YOU SPENT THE WHOLE NIGHT PLANNING WHILE I WAS FINISHING OFF ALL THAT PIZZA THE PLANTS ORDERED, BUT...STILL!"

ESCAPE!
IT'S LIKE ZOMBOSS IS ABLE TO COUNTER OUR EVERY MOVE!
TOTALLY LIED ABOUT THE DOOR!
HERE! THIS WAY!
SAFETY
OR...MAYBE NOT!
SAFETY
GET TO OUR BIKES!
DANG! ZOMBIE BIKE LOCKS! ZOMBOSS IS STILL ONE STEP AHEAD OF US!
HOW'S HE DOING THIS?!

GROCKLE PLORG BLIBBITY FRINGLEBAPPER!
SCREECH
UNCLE DAVE SAID TO GET IN!
AND ALSO TO WIPE YOUR FEET FIRST, BECAUSE YOU STEPPED IN SOMETHING.
AW, MAN.
TWENTY MINUTES LATER.
THANKS FOR SAVING US FROM THE ZOMBIES, CRAZY DAVE.
HRIBBLE FLUMP?
HE...UH... SAYS HE ACTUALLY FORGOT ABOUT THE ZOMBIES.
HE JUST NEEDED US BECAUSE HE FORGOT HOW TO POUR LEMONADE.
IT'S LIKE THIS, UNCLE DAVE.
GAHHH!
POUR
CLAP CLAP CLAP
MMM! LEMONADE. SOOOO GOOD.
HMM? IN THE ICE CUBES. WHAT ARE THESE?

CAMERAS?
HEY! THEY ARE CAMERAS! IN FACT...
UH-OH.
...THERE'S CAMERAS ALL OVER THE HOUSE!
PLUM!
DAVE SAYS HE RECENTLY INVENTED SOMETHING THAT CAN SOLVE THIS PROBLEM. HE SAYS HE'S BEEN WAITING FOR A CHANCE TO USE IT, AND THIS IS PERFECT.
WE CAN BLOCK ALL THE CAMERAS WITH...
"...FLOATING GOLDFISH!"
BLIP BLIP
BLRRP
BLIP BLIP
CURSES!

AND...YOU KNOW, TURN-ABOUT IS FAIR PLAY, SO WE SHOULD PUT CAMERAS INSIDE ZOMBOSS'S HEADQUARTERS.
FIRST WE DISGUISE OURSELVES AS ZOMBIES.
SPLORK
SPLORK
ZOMBIE GREEN
SOON...
ZOMBIES AREN'T VERY SMART, NATE, SO TRY NOT TO ACT SMART.
NOT A PROBLEM!
BRAINS
OKAY. WE'RE IN. JUST PUT THE CAMERAS *EVERYWHERE.*
SHOULDN'T WE HIDE THEM?
PLEASE PAY NO ATTENTION TO THE SECRET CAMERA.
NAWWW. IT'S NOT HARD TO FOOL A ZOMBIE.
BRAINZZ.
BRAINZZ.
BRAINZZ.
UH-OH! ZOMBIE GUARDS, NATE! JUST PLAY ALONG.

BRAINS.
BRAINS.
BRAINS.
BRAINS.
CHOCOLATE PIZZA!
?
?
OOPS.
?

UH, CHOCOLATE BRAIN PIZZA?
GOOD COVER, NATE.
NOW LET'S GET OUT OF HERE.
AND SOON...
YES! IT WORKED!
THE CAMERAS ARE OPERATIONAL. LET'S LEARN ALL THEIR SECRETS.

BURP!
HMM, HAVING INSIDE INFO ON ZOMBIES SITTING AROUND BURPING IS...NOT HELPING.
LOOK, THAT ONE'S STEALING ZOMBOSS'S POP SMARTS!
NIGEL
STILL NOT ALL THAT USEFUL.
WHAT? WHERE DID MY POP SMARTS GO! WHY DOES THIS ALWAYS HAPPEN?
IF I EVER FIND OUT WHO'S STEALING MY POP SMARTS, THEY WILL PAY! PAY!
HMM, ALL WE'VE REALLY LEARNED IS THAT IT'S EASY TO STEAL ZOMBOSS'S BRAIN-FLAVORED POP SMARTS.
KTIK
I...THINK I'LL STICK WITH PEPPERONI-FLAVORED PIZZA.

THE NEXT MORNING...
AND SO, NOW...UTILIZING ALL I'VE LEARNED ABOUT BEING HUMAN, IT'S TIME FOR MY PLAN TO STRIKE TERROR DEEP IN THE HEART OF NEIGHBORVILLE...
...WHICH I WILL DO USING MY NEWFOUND KNOWLEDGE OF HUMANITY...
...AND THEIR LOVE OF PARADES.
YES, A FAKE PARADE TO MOVE MY ZOMBIES INTO POSITION, WITH PARADE FLOATS STUFFED FULL OF ZOMBIES!
BRAINS?
THWAK!
WHMMP!
AS WELL AS ONE PIÑATA THAT'S STUFFED FULL OF ZOMBIES, WHICH I ADMIT I COULD HAVE THOUGHT THROUGH A LITTLE MORE.

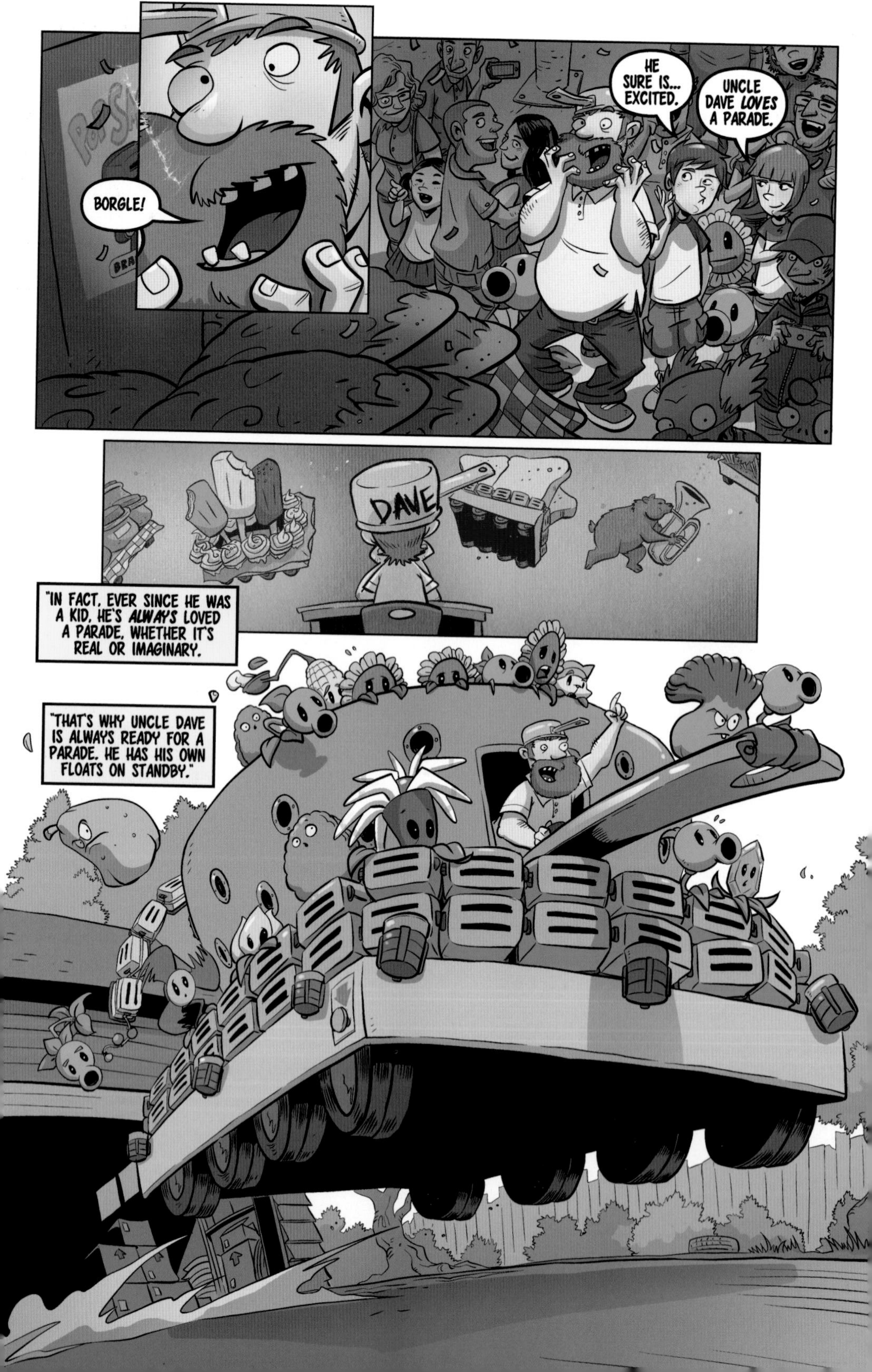
BORGLE!
HE SURE IS... EXCITED.
UNCLE DAVE *LOVES* A PARADE.
DAVE
"IN FACT, EVER SINCE HE WAS A KID, HE'S *ALWAYS* LOVED A PARADE, WHETHER IT'S REAL OR IMAGINARY.
"THAT'S WHY UNCLE DAVE IS ALWAYS READY FOR A PARADE. HE HAS HIS OWN FLOATS ON STANDBY."

BEEP
CRAMTOGGLE
BRREEP
WHAT'S THAT BANNER SAY? MY EYES MUST BE GOING BAD. DOES THAT SAY CRAMTOGGLE...?
CRAMTOGGLE? HIS BANNER DOESN'T MAKE SENSE.
THAT'S BECAUSE IT'S WRITTEN IN DAVE-SPEAK. IT SAYS...
"...PEANUT BUTTER AND JELLY WITH CHEESE.
THOOM
THOOM
THOOM
THOOM
"UNCLE DAVE LOVES IT! I GUESS HE WANTS TO GIVE EVERYONE A TREAT."
PAFF!
THORK!
WHUPP!
FLORNK!

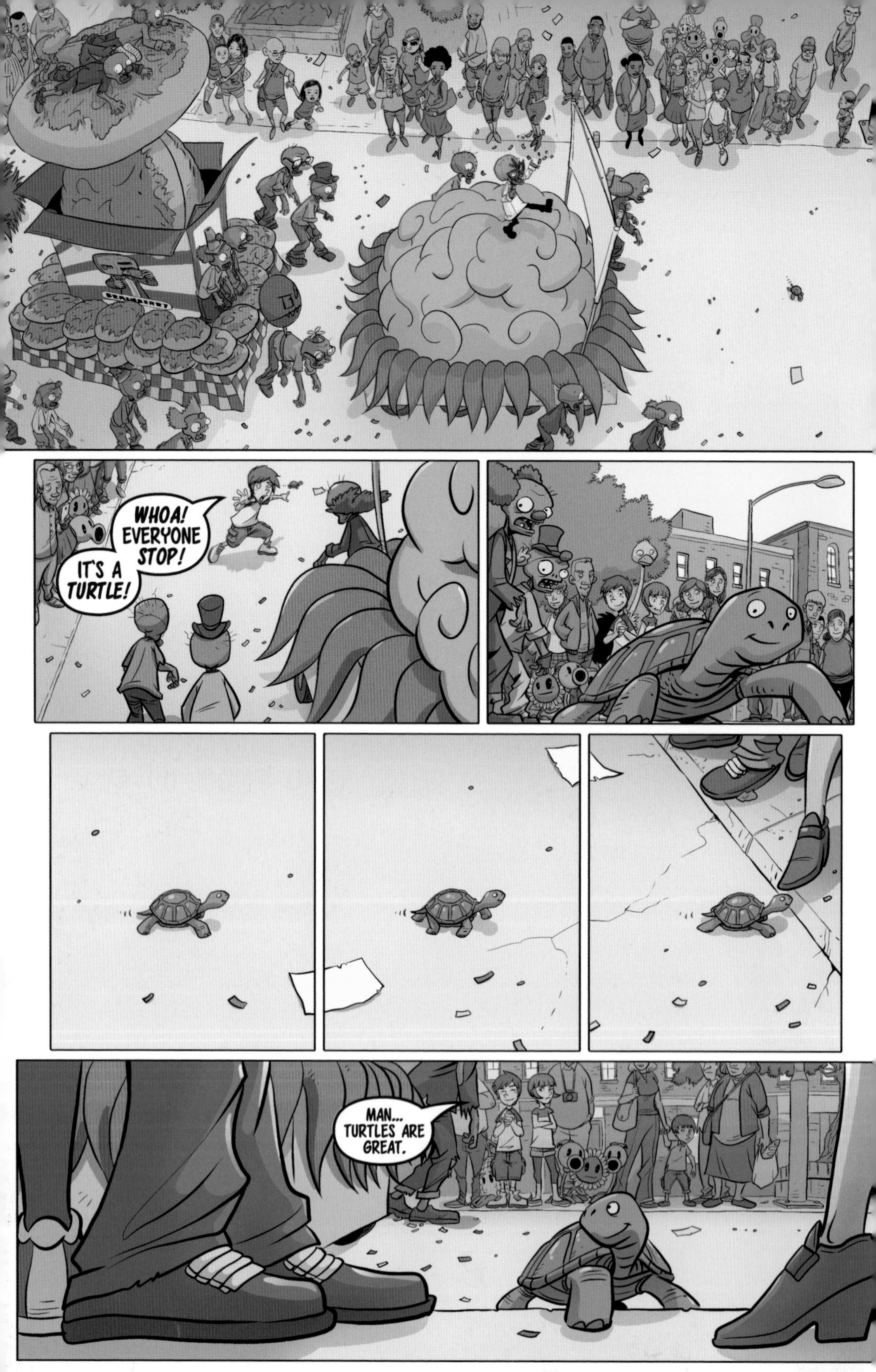
WHOA! EVERYONE STOP!
IT'S A TURTLE!
MAN... TURTLES ARE GREAT.

NOW, SHALL WE RESUME OUR CONTEST?
IT'S TIME TO PROVE THAT ZOMBIES ARE THE BEST AT ANYTHING! EVEN AT... ACTING HUMAN!
YOU'RE ON! THERE'S NO WAY YOU COULD BEAT A HUMAN AT ACTING HUMAN!
I'LL SHOW YOU HOW HUMANS ACT! I'LL--
OW! HE HIT ME! I'M HITTING HIM!
YOU SAID MY EARS WERE STINKY!
STOP IT, YOU TWO!
SORRY! THEY'RE ALWAYS DOING THAT. BUT BOYS WILL BE BOYS, RIGHT?
THAT'S JUST HOW PEOPLE ACT!
HMM... INTERESTING.
THAT'S HOW PEOPLE ACT, EHH?
FIGHT!

ROUND ONE!
FROGPANTS VS. FRED THE SUNFLOWER
ZOMBIES WIN!

ROUND TWO!
BALLOON ZOMBIES VS. ANTI-GRAVITY GOLDFISH!
IT'S A DRAW!

ROUND THREE!
NIGEL BLIMPBOTTOM VS. JEFF THE BLOOMERANG!
THWIP
THUMP
THWIP
THUMP
PLANTS WIN!

TUGBOAT-
PUNCH
PUNCH
PUNCH
PUNCH
PUNCH
PUNCH
PUNCH
ROUND FOUR!
TUGBOAT VS. GRRAWRR-BEAR THE ULTIMATE FACE-PUNCHER!
PLANTS WIN!

ROUND FIVE!
MR. STUBBINS VS. A PEANUT BUTTER AND JELLY WITH CHEESE SANDWICH!
NOM NOM NOM
ZOMBIES WIN!

ROUND SIX!
NATE TIMELY VS. GARGANTUAR!
WHAT? WHOA! SKIP TO ROUND SEVEN!
ZOMBIES WIN!

ROUND SEVEN!
PATRICE BLAZING AND THREE HUNDRED AND FIFTY-SEVEN FEET OF DUCT TAPE VS. A CONEHEAD ZOMBIE!
BRAINS?
PLANTS WIN!

ROUND EIGHT!
ZOMBIES VS. DOORKNOB!
?
?
BRAINS?
?
PLANTS WIN!

ROUND NINE!
ZOMBIE VS. TRICYCLE!
GIVE HIM A SECOND! HE'S GETTING THE HANG OF IT!
PLANTS WIN!

ROUND TEN!
CRAZY DAVE VS. ZOMBOSS! PARADE FLOAT BATTLE!
HMM! THIS BATTLE HAS STARTED TO TURN AGAINST ME, BUT...THIS WILL BE WHERE MY VICTORY IS WON!
THIS WILL BE WHERE NEIGHBORVILLE FALLS, BECAUSE I...

...HAVE FILLED MY FLOAT FULL OF ZOMBIES.

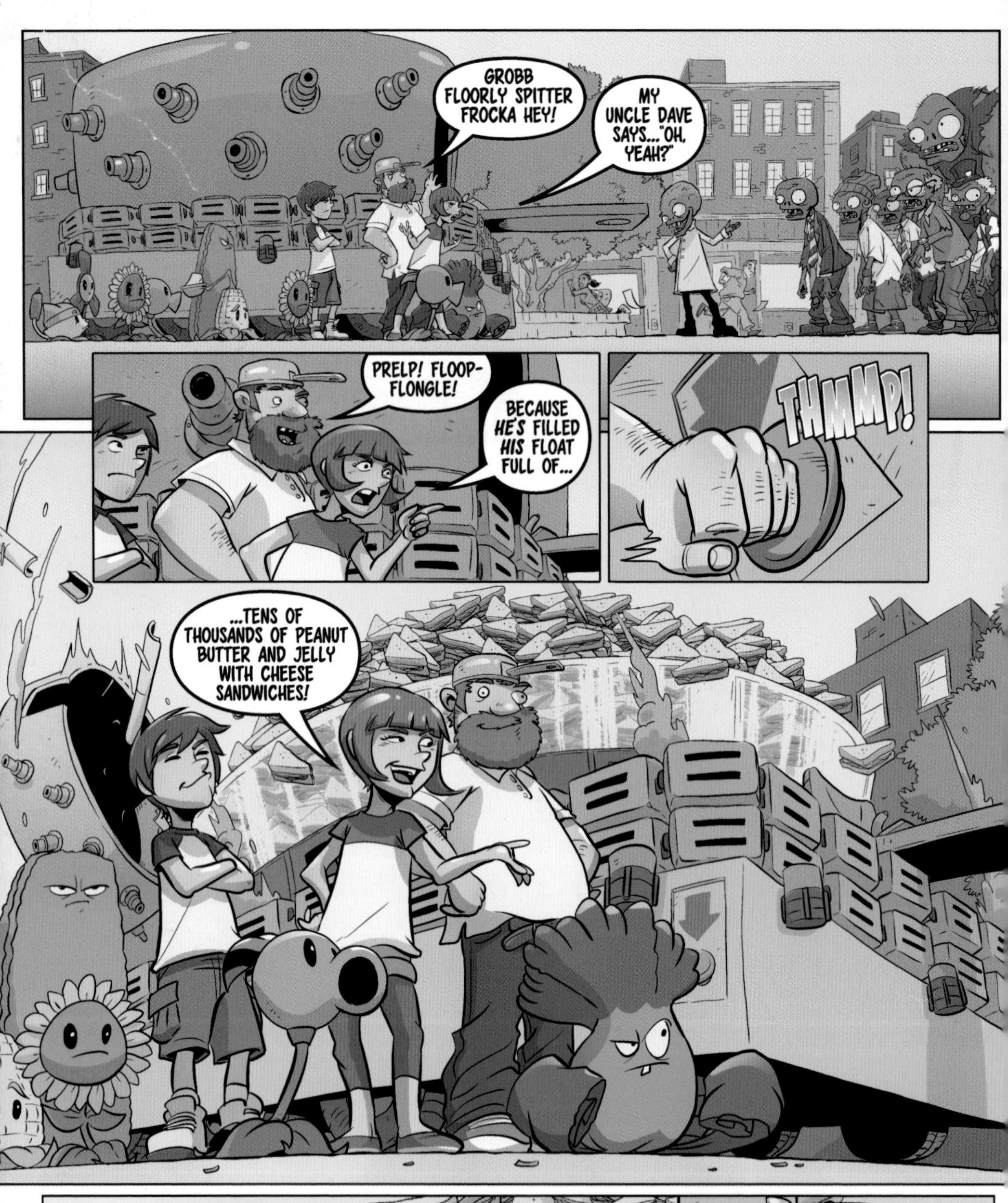
GROBB FLOORLY SPITTER FROCKA HEY!
MY UNCLE DAVE SAYS..."OH, YEAH?"
PRELP! FLOOP-FLONGLE!
BECAUSE *HE'S* FILLED *HIS* FLOAT FULL OF...
THMMP!
...TENS OF THOUSANDS OF PEANUT BUTTER AND JELLY WITH CHEESE SANDWICHES!

WAIT. WHAT?
OH, WE ARE SO DOOMED.

DOOM!
DOOM!
DOOM!
THOOP
PAFF!
THOOP
PAFF!
THOOP
PAFF!
SANDWICHES!
MUNCH
MUNCH
DOOM!
MUNCH
MUNCH
MUNCH
SERIOUSLY, THE MESSAGE HERE IS...
DOOM!

AND SO, BECAUSE OF MY GENIUS, BECAUSE OF MY DESTINY, BECAUSE OF A LITTLE BIT OF CHEATING, VICTORY IS...MINE!
THE YUMMY HUMANS ARE MINE! THE PLANTS WILL BE DESTROYED!
HMM. YOU KNOW WHAT?
I FEEL LIKE INDULGING IN A LITTLE BIT OF MANIACAL LAUGHTER.
HA HA HA HA HA! HEH HEH! HA HA HA! HAAA! HA HA!
SQUICK SQUICK SQUICK SQUICK!
THIS... IS BAD.
I KNOW! WE'RE NO MATCH FOR THIS MANY ZOMBIES, ESPECIALLY WITH THE POWER OF THOSE GARGANTUARS AND ZOMBOSS'S EVIL GENIUS...
HA HA HA HA HA!
...AND THOSE THREE GUYS THAT STOLE ZOMBOSS'S POP SMARTS.
HA HAAA! HA...HA... UHH...?

WAIT. SAY WHAT AGAIN?
FROGPANTZZ.
THOSE GUYS. WE SAW THEM STEAL YOUR POP SMARTS.
ON CAMERA.
NIGEL
DESTROY THEM!
DESTROY NIGEL BLIMPBOTTOM!
DESTROY FROGPANTS!
DESTROY TUGBOAT!
THIRTY MINUTES LATER...
ARE THEY... JUST GOING TO KEEP DOING THAT?
LOOKS THAT WAY. I WONDER IF WE COULD ROUND THEM UP WHILE THEY'RE DISTRACTED?
TWAK
NIGEL
KEEP DESTROYING!
THUMP
MORE DESTROYING!
SMACK
BRAINZZ?
TWO HOURS LATER...
KEEP DESTROYING!
WOW. WE HAVE MOST OF THEM ROUNDED UP NOW, BUT...THE OTHERS ARE STILL GOING AT IT.
TWAK
THUMP
SMACK
HMM. I STILL FEEL WE HAVE NOT TRULY DESTROYED THEM!
BRAINZZ!

AND SO...THREE HOURS LATER.
SEE? THAT'S ONE OF THE MOST IMPORTANT LESSONS YOU CAN LEARN ABOUT BEING HUMAN...OUR SENSE OF COOPERATION.
IF ZOMBOSS AND HIS ZOMBIES HAD WORKED TOGETHER, THEY WOULD HAVE WON!
THAT'S RIGHT! NOW...IF NOBODY MINDS, I'LL HAVE THIS LAST SLICE OF PIZZA.
REACH!
SLAP!
GRRRRR...
HEY! THAT'S MINE!
YOU GIVE THAT BACK!
THMMP! THMMP! GRRRRRR!
GRRRRR!
C'MON! IT'S PEPPERONI!
NiGEL
ZOMBOSS IZ A GERK!
ZOMBOSS UNFAIRZZ!
WE NEEDZ A PLACE OF OUR OWNZ.
THE END.

PLANTS
VS.
ZOMBIES
™
ZOMBOSS

PETAL TO THE METAL

Written by PAUL TOBIN

Art by RON CHAN

Colors by MATT J. RAINWATER

Letters by STEVE DUTRO

Plants vs. Zombies comic #7 cover art (previous page) by Ron Chan

PLING
PLING
PLING

HUH. WELL, LOOK AT THAT, SKIDDOO. A LIZARD ON MY SHOE.
AIN'T THAT 'BOUT THE MOST DANGEDEST THING YA EVER SAW?

YEP.
LIZARD ON MY SHOE.
NOW WE SEEN IT ALL.
GAS

ERRRRT!!!

?

UM, HELLO IN THERE. YOU LOOKING TO GETCHA SOME GAS?
NO. WE'RE LOOKING FOR...

...BRAINNSSS...
GAS
STU
ZOMBOSS

FOUR DAYS EARLIER...
BRAAAAAINS?
GNAW
GNAW
GNAW

SO...YOU'RE A REPORTER FOR BRAIN Z, THE WEEKLY BLOG ABOUT ALL THINGS ZOMBIE?
PRESS
BRAINZZZ.

COME THIS WAY. I'LL SHOW YOU MY LATEST INNOVATIONS.
OH, BUT...WATCH YOUR HEAD. I'M TRYING OUT A NEW TRAINING SYSTEM.
testing
THOOP
WHAP
THOOP
THOOP

OF LATE, WE'VE BEEN HAVING TROUBLE WITH SPIKEWEEDS DESTROYING OUR TIRES, BUT MY BRILLIANT MIND HAS DEVISED A SOLUTION!
PRESS
brainz
Pop!

BIG, FAT TIRES!
BRAINSSS.
BRAINSSS.
TIRESSS.

ALSO... METAL TIRES!
AND IMP TIRES!
BRAINSSS?
CRANKITY CRUNCH

EVEN CARS WITH NO TIRES!
ALTHOUGH THE LAST ONE DOESN'T WORK VERY WELL, ACTUALLY...
WHRRRR
WHRRR
WHRRRR

WE'RE ALSO EXPERIMENTING WITH SPIKE SCOOPERS, AND...
PRESS
WHAPPP!
WHAPPP!

...THESE SPECIAL RUBBER SUITS THAT ALLOW MY ZOMBIES TO SIMPLY LEAP ON THE SPIKE TRAPS, WITH NO HARM.

PRESS
THUMP

YOU'RE SUPPOSED TO PUT THE SUIT ON FIRST.
BRAAAAAAINSSS..

AS SOON AS WE WORK OUT ALL THESE MINOR PROBLEMS, WE WILL RULE THE STREETS!
AND THOSE WHO RULE THE STREETS RULE THE CITY!
AND THOSE WHO RULE THE CITY... RULE THE CITY!
PRESS

ALTHOUGH I SUPPOSE THAT LAST BIT IS REDUNDANT.

BUT HERE...HERE... IS THE START OF MY NEW ARMY!
AN ARMY OF RACECAR DRIVERS AND ZOMBIE MECHANICS!

THE WORLD RECORD FOR A PIT STOP IS ELEVEN SECONDS, BUT MY TRAINED ZOMBIES CAN DO A FULL PIT STOP IN ONLY...
THOK

CLKK
CLKK
CLKK

SHUNK!
PRESS
CLKK
CLKK
CLKK

PRESS
CLKK
CLKK
CLKK

...TWELVE MINUTES AND SEVEN SECONDS!
BRAAAAINS.
PRESS
CTICK!

MEANWHILE...
!
LOOK OUT FOR THAT DUCK!

AAAH!
!!!
OH, NO!

FAILEd
FAILEd

AW, ANOTHER FAILED GRADE.
IT'S HARD TO TEACH PLANTS HOW TO DRIVE WHEN WE DON'T KNOW HOW TO DO IT OURSELVES.
WHY WAS THERE A DUCK ON A HANG GLIDER?
GAME OVER

I WISH I COULD CONVINCE MY UNCLE TO HELP TEACH THE PLANTS. BUT THAT'S NOT HAPPENING.

"AT LEAST NOT UNTIL HE GETS THE HIGH SCORE ON DON'T BLINK."
DON'T BLINK

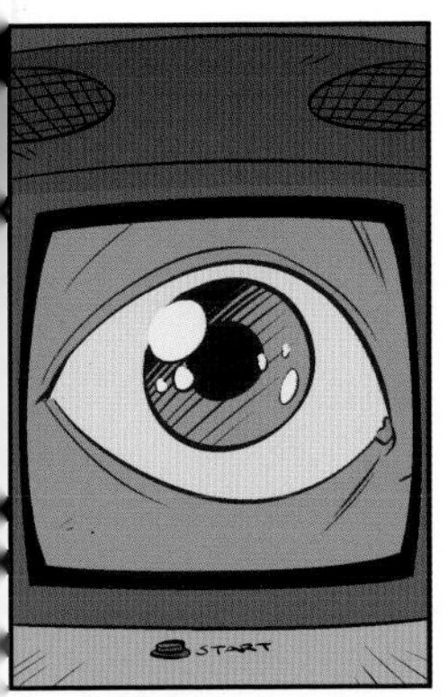
START

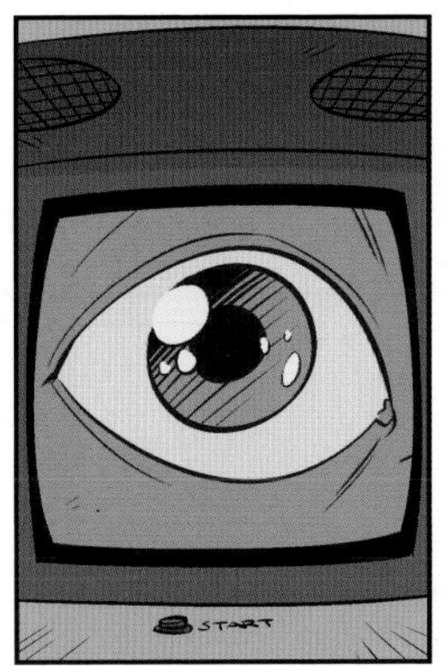
START

TREMBLE

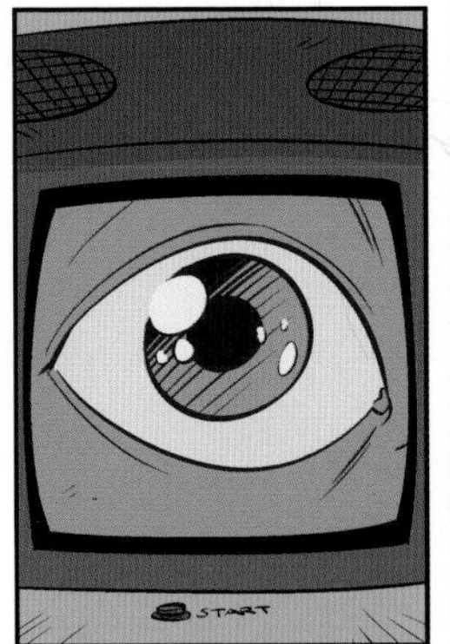
START

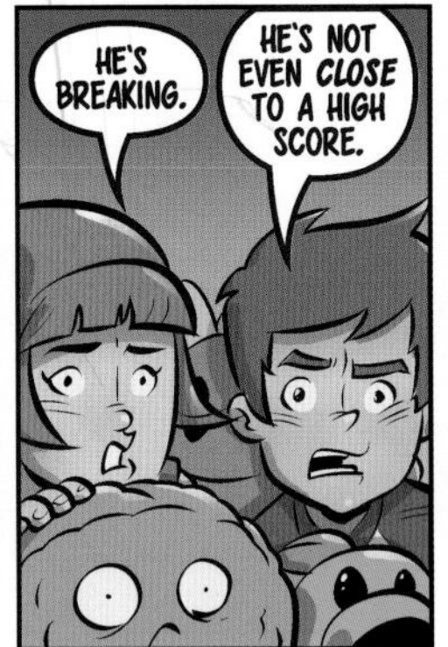
HE'S BREAKING.
HE'S NOT EVEN *CLOSE* TO A HIGH SCORE.

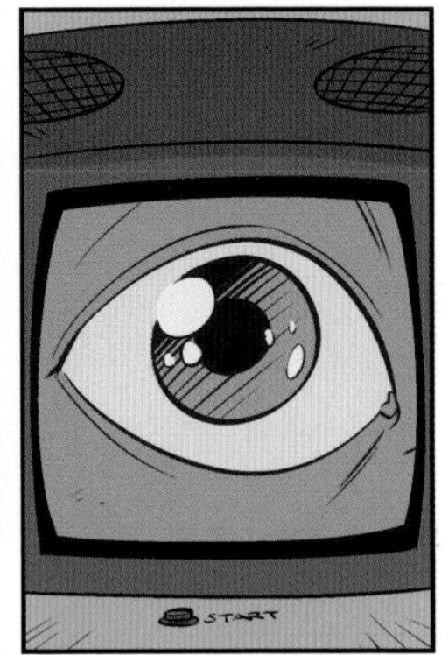
START

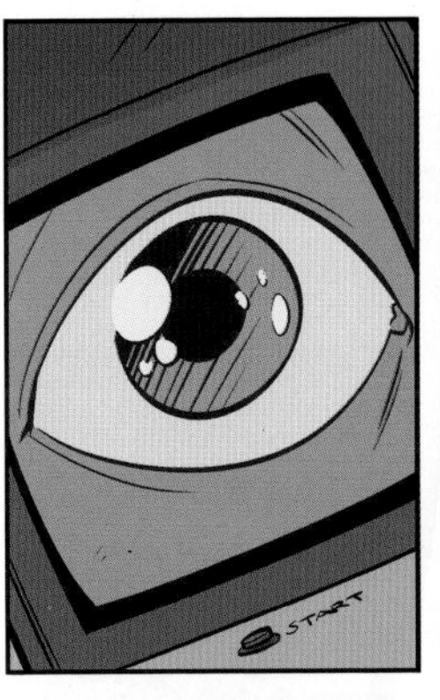
START

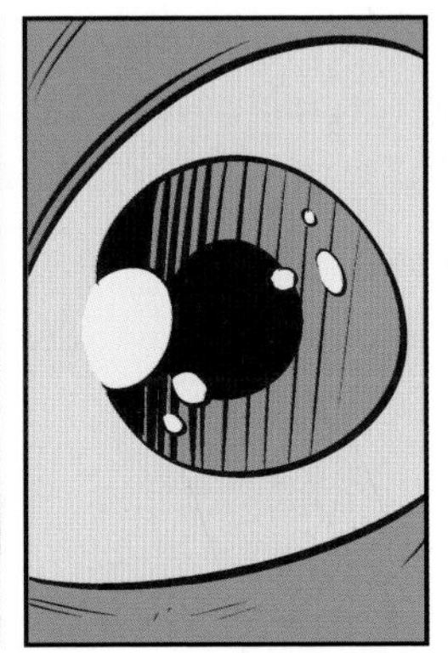

TREMBLE
QUIVER
TREMOR

BLINK

MACHINE WINS!

OM FLONGLE.

C'MON, DAVE, MAYBE YOU CAN COME BACK LATER?
PRACTICE IN THE MEANTIME?
YOU LOSE!

THE THING IS, WE COULD REALLY USE YOUR HELP.
WE'RE HAVING TROUBLE TRAINING THE PLANTS. THIS DRIVING GAME ISN'T WORKING.
CAN'T YOU BUILD A GOOD CAR THEY COULD USE?

HMMM?

GRAMLOG FLOGGLE!

AND SO...
BANG!
SMAKK!
SPRANK!
FLOONT!
PLORNNG!

AND THEN...
UNCLE DAVE, UM...COULD YOU JUST MAKE A REGULAR CAR?
I DON'T THINK IT NEEDS A BUFFALO-TOSSING CATAPULT.
SLORG RA!

OR AN ICE-CREAM MACHINE.
WAIT! IS THAT A MACHINE THAT MAKES ICE-CREAM MACHINES? WE NEED THAT!!!
PLONG!
CLONNK

MEANWHILE...
HEH HEH HEH!

MY ZOMBIE MECHANICS ARE GETTING COMPETITIVE.
LOOK AT THESE CARS!
Z35

LOOK! IT'S A FIFTY-IMP-POWER ENGINE!
BRAINS?
BRAINS?
BRAINS?

AHHHHH...
BRAINS!
BRAINS!
COMPETITION IS GETTING FIERCE!

LET'S ADD IN THIS ENGINE!
CLINK-CLANK!

AND THIS ONE.

AND THIS ONE.

AND THESE TWO.

YOU CAN'T HAVE TOO MANY ENGINES!

BRAAAINSS!
THOOM THOOM THOOM

YES! WE HAVE ACHIEVED...
STOMP
STOMP
STOMP
THOOM
THOOM

...FULL GARGANTUAR POWER!

YES! CARS FOR ALL MY ZOMBIES.
FOR TOO LONG, MY ZOMBIE HORDE HAS DONE NOTHING BUT...
...SIMPLY SHUFFLE ALONG! BUT NOW, WE WILL HAVE...
SHUFFLE
SHUFFLE
SHUFFLE
"...SPEED!"
ZOOM!

LET ME INTRODUCE THE CARS!
THIS ONE'S KNOWN AS THE BLACK TORNADO--THE CAR WITH A TORNADO FOR AN ENGINE!

AND... HERE! THE ZOMBIE SLEDGE-RAMMER!

AND THIS IS... DOOM-STUART!
NAMED AFTER STUART, THERE.
BRAINS.
STUART
STU

STU
IN THE SPIRIT OF COMPETITION, I HEREBY ANNOUNCE... A RACE!
THE BEST CARS AND THE BEST ZOMBIES WILL COMPETE TO WIN THE GRAND PRIZE OF...

"...ONE FULL MINUTE OF TIME WITH MY AUTOMATIC ZOMBOSS HAND-SHAKING MACHINE!
"AND AN AUTOGRAPHED PICTURE OF...ME!

"LOSERS WILL GET THREE DAYS WITH MY AUTOMATIC BOOT-KICKING MACHINE."
BOOT!
"AND AN AUTOGRAPHED PICTURE OF ME."

I WILL ALSO GET AN AUTOGRAPHED PICTURE OF ME.

I JUST...REALLY LIKE THEM.

LET THE RACE BEGIN!

ONLY MINUTES LATER...
CAREFUL CROSSING THE STREET, PRINCESS WAILTIME.
YIP! YAP!
YIP! YAP!
Welcome to the bucolic streets of
Neighborville!
The city known for peace, friendly citizens, and quiet enjoyment.

BRNZZZ
RRRROAR!
Welcome to the bucolic streets of
Neighbor
The city known for peace
citizens, and
Alzo, the okazional Zombie Invazion!!
SCREEAA!
VZOOOOM

AHHH!

AHHH! AGAIN!

PRINCESS WAILTIME?

YIP!

AND...
IS THIS THAT AMNESIA AVENUE SOAP OPERA?
I HATE THIS SHOW. CHANGE THE CHANNEL!

KRAAASH!

GOOD ENOUGH.

BRAINS!
WHOOSH
BRAINS!
OH, NO! ZOMBIES! WHAT COULD POSSIBLY BE WORSE?
HONNK!
ROAR
SCREECH

VWRRRR
THUPP

GAH! MY TOE!
GAH! A ZOMBIE HEDGEHOG!

STRUBBLE?
HOP!
HOP!
HOP!

STEP!
STEP!
STEP!

ZOOOOOSH!
RRRROAR!
IRRROOM!

AH, CRAZY DAVE.
I SUSPECTED HE'D SHOW.
FROGPANTZZZ.

ERRRRT!

LORPPLE GLORN LOG SPLARN!
UNCLE DAVE ASKS...

...DO YOU HAVE ANY BUBBLEGUM?

AND, UH... ALSO...

HE CHALLENGES YOU!

GROBBLE CRUNCHY PLOPPLE FUZZ-TOWER LOOOGFREN!
HE CHALLENGES YOU IN THE NAME OF ALL THAT IS *GOOD*, IN THE NAME OF *ICE CREAM*, AND *SUNFLOWERS*, AND *DONKEY EARS!*
AND HE CHALLENGES YOU FOR THE SCIENTIFICALLY SOUND REASON OF...*DUH.*

CAR AGAINST CAR! *LOSER* HAS TO LEAVE THIS CITY *FOREVER!*

YOU'RE ON.

LET THE RACES BEGIN!!
SUN-POWERED CARS VS. IMP-POWERED CARS!

IN THIS CORNER...THE ICE-CREAM RACER--SPONSORED BY TWIDDY-DINKIES GARDEN SUPPLY!
AND IN THIS CORNER...ZOMBOSS'S CARS--SPONSORED BY POP SMARTS!
VS
TWIDDYDINKIES
GARDEN SUPPLY
POP SMARTS
THE TASTY BRAIN TREAT!
NEIGHBORVILLE FLAVORED
BOSS

AND NOW... RACE!
WAVE
WAVE
WAVE

RACE!!
VRRRROOOOOM!
RACE!!

RACE!!
OKAY, NOW THAT'S THE DANGEDEST THING I EVER SAW.
GAS
WAVE WAVE WAVE
Vacation!
BRAINSSSS!
SNAP
SNAP
SNAP
SNAP
SNAP
SNAP
SNAP
SNAP
SNAP
SNAP
Echo Canyon

RACE!!

RACE!!

YOU WILL NEVER DEFEAT MY MAGNIFICENT RACECARS!
MY DRIVERS NEVER NEED SLEEP! THEY NEED NO REST! NOTHING WILL STOP US!
THERE ARE NO DISTRACTIONS THAT--
RACE!!

CLANG
CLANG CLANGITTY
CLANG

OOOH! MY POP SMARTS ARE READY!
I'LL HAVE TO CONTINUE MY MANIACAL RANT AFTER MY SNACKY-SNACKS!

I CAN'T BELIEVE I'M SAYING THIS, BUT...ZOMBOSS IS *RIGHT*.
WE'VE BEEN GOING FOR HOURS AND HOURS NOW, AND SOONER OR LATER, WE'LL NEED SLEEP.

FLURNT! *FLOOSWHISTLE!*
UNCLE DAVE SAYS *HE* HASN'T SLEPT IN FIFTEEN YEARS, AND IT HASN'T AFFECTED *HIM* AT ALL.

GRAWS BAGGLE.

HMMM.

RIGHT, SO WE CAN SLEEP IN SHIFTS.
YOU GO FIRST.

SHINE!

SHINE!

I'M SORRY, DO YOU MIND?
SHINE!
SHINE!

RACE!!
WE'RE LOSING THIS RACE!
THROW MORE IMPS INTO THE ENGINE!
barrel o' imps!
ZOMBOSS

WE'RE WINNING!
OUT HERE IN THE DESERT, WE HAVE SO MUCH SUN POWER!
RACE!!

ROADSIDE ATTRACTIONS!
WHOA. THIS IS... AMAZING.
AH, NATE, WE REALLY SHOULD GET GOING.
WORLD'S LARGEST DINO-PIG SCULPTURE!

RACE!!
FASTER! FASTER!
WHOEVER LOSES THIS RACE IS BANNED FROM NEIGHBORVILLE FOREVER!

TIME OUT!
STOP
DOINK
DOINK
DOINK
DECIDING WHY THE CHICKEN WANTED TO CROSS THE ROAD!

GOING TO THE MOVIES?
BAND PRACTICE?
MAYBE A WORM?
ANYBODY SEE ANY WORMS?
BRAINS?
BRAINSSS?
BRAINS?
BRAINS?
to vizit his mom?

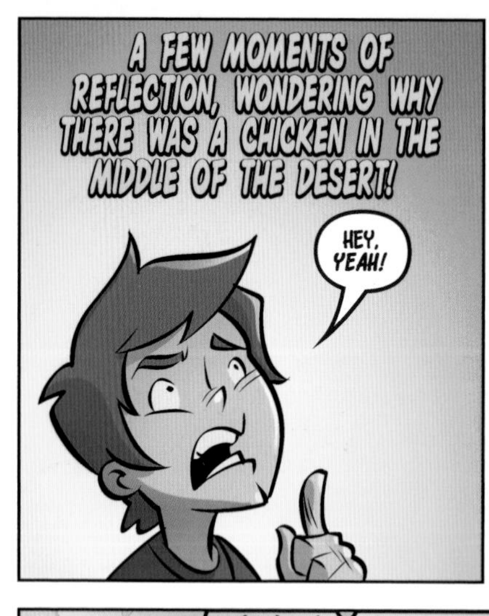
A FEW MOMENTS OF REFLECTION, WONDERING WHY THERE WAS A CHICKEN IN THE MIDDLE OF THE DESERT!
HEY, YEAH!

RACE!!
OH, NO! ZOMBOSS HAS A CLOUD MACHINE! WE'LL LOSE SUN POWER!

HA HAAA! I THINK OF EVERYTHING!
THERE IS NOTHING THAT ESCAPES MY GENIUS MIND!

WAIT, HAS ANYONE SEEN MR. STUBBINS?
HAS HE ESCAPED?

MILES AWAY...
ZOOOOOOOOOM!

RACE!!

Competitive squirrel naming!
florence
alex-ander the alien axe maztr
carl
SQUIRBLE

A Sasquatch sighting!
OOF?

AAARRR?!
NO! WE'RE NOT GOING BACK TO SEE SASQUATCH.
NO! I DON'T CARE IF HE'S YOUR COUSIN!
NO! I DON'T CARE IF HE'S HAVING A BIRTHDAY PARTY!
NO! YOU CAN'T DRIVE!

HEY, ZOMBOSS! WE'RE TOTALLY WINNING THIS RACE!
HEH HEH! YOU THINK SO, DO YOU?
YOU FOOLISH MORTAL--WITH YOUR TINY BUT TASTY BRAIN! DON'T YOU SEE? YOU'VE FALLEN INTO MY INGENIOUS TRAP!
ALL THESE TIMES I'VE TRIED TO DESTROY NEIGHBORVILLE? CRAZY DAVE AND YOU KIDS ARE THE ONLY ONES WHO EVER STOPPED ME.

"BUT NOW, I'VE CLEVERLY DRAWN YOU HUNDREDS OF MILES FROM THE CITY, AND IT WILL BE MINE! MINE!!
"THE DAY OF THE ZOMBIE IS HERE!"

OH, NO! YOU KNOW WHAT THIS MEANS?
YES! WE HAVE TO GET BACK TO THE CITY--FAST--OR EVERYTHING WILL BE DESTROYED!
THE REAL RACE FOR NEIGHBORVILLE HAS JUST BEGUN! WE CAN'T STOP FOR ANYTHING!

ERRRRT
SCREEEECH

HEY, YOU THINK THAT...AS LONG AS WE'RE GOING THIS WAY...WE COULD STOP OFF AND SEE THAT DINO-PIG AGAIN?

FRIENDSHIP BRACELET EMPORIUM
STOP
Polly's Posh Pancakes
NEIGHBORVILLE, THE CITY OF SMILING FRIENDS, WHERE PEOPLE GATHER TOGETHER FOR SUCH SIMPLE PASTIMES AS...

PLAYING BADMINTON!
INCOMING!
OH, JOLLY GOOD SHOT!

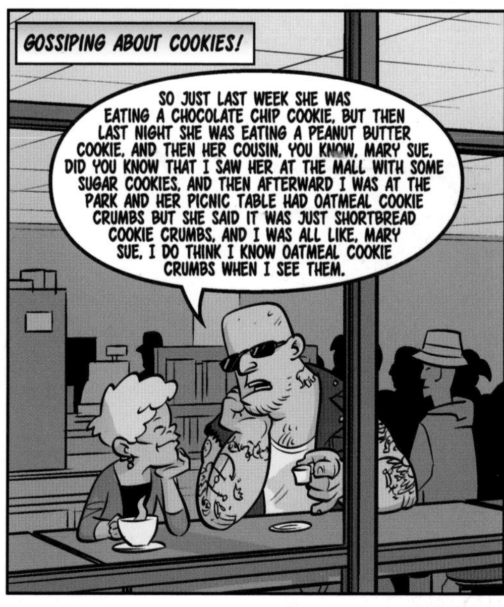
GOSSIPING ABOUT COOKIES!
SO JUST LAST WEEK SHE WAS EATING A CHOCOLATE CHIP COOKIE, BUT THEN LAST NIGHT SHE WAS EATING A PEANUT BUTTER COOKIE, AND THEN HER COUSIN, YOU KNOW, MARY SUE, DID YOU KNOW THAT I SAW HER AT THE MALL WITH SOME SUGAR COOKIES, AND THEN AFTERWARD I WAS AT THE PARK AND HER PICNIC TABLE HAD OATMEAL COOKIE CRUMBS BUT SHE SAID IT WAS JUST SHORTBREAD COOKIE CRUMBS, AND I WAS ALL LIKE, MARY SUE, I DO THINK I KNOW OATMEAL COOKIE CRUMBS WHEN I SEE THEM.

GOING ON CAT-WATCHING EXPEDITIONS!
IS THAT A SPECKLED SNOOZER?
WELL, IT COULD BE, BUT IT LOOKS MORE LIKE A SPOTTED DAYTIME NAPPER TO ME.

SELLING HOMEMADE LEMONADE!
it's Lemonade!
all proceeds go to the Handshake Academy
LEMONADE! ONLY A DOLLAR!
IT'S FOR A GOOD CAUSE!

AND ALSO GETTING INVADED BY ZOMBIES.
FRIENDSHIP BRACELET EMPORIUM
STOP
Polly's Posh Pancakes

AND SO...
INCOMING!
OH, THIS IS WRETCHED!

AND ALSO...
NO! STAY AWAY FROM MY COOKIE COLLECTION!
NOOOOO!

PLUS...
LOOK OUT! IT'S A FINE SPECIMEN OF A RED-TIED BRAIN GRABBER!
AND THERE'S A LOOMING CLUB THUMPER!

WORST OF ALL...
it's Lemonade!
all proceeds go to the
brainz

WITH A FINAL RESULT OF...
WE NEED HELP!

BUT...PATRICE BLAZING ISN'T HOME!

AND...NATHAN TIMELY ISN'T HOME!
ROOM

AND...THE PLANTS ARE OUT OF TOWN!
PLANT FOOD

AND CRAZY DAVE IS GONE, WHICH ALL MEANS...
SANDWICH!!

THERE'S NOBODY TO STOP US!
NOW THAT WE'VE LURED THAT CRETINOUS CRAZY DAVE AND THOSE TWICE-CURSED CHILDREN OUT OF THE CITY, TAKING CONTROL OF NEIGHBORVILLE WILL BE SO EASY!

GATHER AROUND AND LISTEN, AS I EXPLAIN... IN A SIMPLE, STEP-BY-STEP MANNER...EXACTLY HOW WE'RE GOING TO DO IT!

"FIRST, WE RELEASE SOME ZOMBOSS BALLOONS IN ORDER TO INSPIRE FEAR!

"FEAR IN MY WORKERS, TO MOTIVATE THEM!"
TAP
TAP
THOOP
BRAINZZZ.

"AND FEAR IN THE TOWNSPEOPLE, BECAUSE IT'S FUN TO TERRIFY THEM!"
GLOBOPHOBIA
SUPPORT NETWOR

AND THE NEXT STEP!
BY FAR THE MOST IMPORTANT STEP IS...

ZZZRRRK

NiGeL

ZOMBOSS SPECIAL
ALERT TV SCREEN
DO NOT
UNPLUG!!

NiGeL

NiGeL
BRAINSSSS.

BRAINZZ.
BRAINS.
BRAINZZ.
BRAINZZ.
BRAINS.
BRAINSSS.
SHUFFLE
SHUFFLE
SHUFFLE
SHUFFLE
SHUFFLE
SHUFFLE
SHUFFLE

MEANWHILE...OODLES OF MILES AWAY...
ICE-CREAM RACER!!!
GRIPPLE FLOOP FLOUNDERGRAM?

WHAT'S HE SAYING?
HE WANTS TO KNOW IF WE'RE STAYING AHEAD OF THE ZOMBIES.

YEAH! I THINK SO!
LUCKILY, THEY'RE WAY BACK THERE, AND...

"...OUR SUN-POWERED CAR DOES GREAT IN THE DESERT, BUT...

"...WE STILL HAVE TO KEEP MOVING!"

DO WE HAVE TIME TO STOP FOR THE WORLD'S THIRD-BEST PIZZA?
WORLD'S THIRD-BEST PIZZA!
NO!
DO WE HAVE TIME TO RAMP THINGS?
SUPER COOL RAMP!
NO!
DO WE HAVE TIME TO STOP FOR THE WORLD'S SECOND-BEST PIZZA?
WORLD'S SECOND-BEST PIZZA
IT'S...TOO TWO GOOD!
NO!
A.P. ZAA
Totally worth it...
DO WE HAVE TIME FOR ME TO ASK YOU WHERE CRAZY DAVE WENT?
NO!
WAIT, WHAT?
OH, NO!
CRAZY DAVE! WHERE ARE YOU?

WE DON'T HAVE TIME TO LOOK FOR HIM! WE HAVE TO KEEP GOING!
BUT... WE CAN'T DRIVE!

WE'LL HAVE TO LET ONE OF THE PLANTS DRIVE!
WHAT? BUT THEY CAN'T DRIVE EITHER!
NO CHOICE! WE HAVE TO GET BACK TO NEIGHBORVILLE! AND WE CAN'T DO THAT IF WE DON'T STAY AHEAD OF...

SLEDGE-RAMMER!!!
?!

BLACK TORNADO!!!

DOOM-STUART!!!
SUPER COOL RAMP!
WAVE WAVE
SNAP

EANWHILE, THE ZOMBIES ARE LOST AND NEED DIRECTIONS HOME!

BRAINSSSS?

OH BOY! THERE'S PIZZA AHEAD!
BRAINZ?

BRAINSSSS?

BRAINS?

MEANWHILE...
UM, PATRICE? WHO'S THAT GUY IN THE BACK SEAT?

OTTO
IT'S... A ROBOT, I THINK?
THERE'S A NOTE FROM UNCLE DAVE!

IT SAYS THE ROBOT'S NAME IS OTTO PILOT. HE CAN DRIVE THE CAR!
SO UNCLE DAVE DIDN'T LEAVE US STRANDED!

THERE! BUCKLE HIM IN! SWITCH HIM ON!
OKAY! OKAY!
OTTO

HE HAS THREE SPEEDS. WHICH ONE SHOULD I CHOOSE?
THERE'S... TOO FAST. RECKLESS. AND SURPRISE.
LET'S TRY TOO FAST, SINCE I DON'T THINK WE CAN GO TOO FAST RIGHT NOW, NOT WITH ALL THE ZOMBIES CATCHING UP!
OFF
TOO FAST
RECKLESS
SURPRISE!

TOOOOOO FASSSSST!
I'LL TRY THE RECKLESS SETTING!
FWOOSH

AHHHH! TRY THE SURPRISE SETTING!
THUMP THUMP THUMPITTY-THUMP

OH. THIS ISN'T SO BAD.
OTTO

SURPRISE!
HUH?

ZOOOOOOOMERS!

WELL, THAT CERTAINLY WAS A SURPRISE.

MEANWHILE, BACK IN NEIGHBORVILLE...
BANG!
BANG!
BANG!
BANG!

AND...
PFF!
PFF!
PFF!

BRAINZZZ...

Zombosz

BRAINSSSS...

BAAA-RAINSSS...
MUNCH MUNCH

YaYYY Zomboss!
WELL COME
HOMb
Zombosz
brainsss
FrogPants

OKAY. FRED'S THE BEST DRIVER WE HAVE.
HE SHOULD BE ABLE TO GET US BACK TO NEIGHBORVILLE.

GOOD, BECAUSE WE'VE BEEN RACING FOR OVER A DAY, AND I'M SO...I'M SO...SLEEPY, I'M...I'M...ZZZZZZZ...

WAKE UP!

HUH? CHESTBEARD?
HOW'D YOU GET HERE IN...

...OUR CAR?
LISTEN, YOU SCURVY DOG... YOU'RE GOING ABOUT THIS RACE ALL WRONG!
TAKE A LESSON FROM CHESTBEARD THE PIRATE--THE WAY TO WIN A RACE IS TO...

...BOARD THE OTHER SHIPS IN THE RACE...
...AND FIND THE KNAVES WHO'VE BEEN BEDEVILING YE...
...AND GIVE THEM A SUPLEX!
WHAM
GAH!
WHAT'S UP, NATE?
OH. I THINK I HAD...A DREAM?
THERE WAS CHESTBEARD, AND A PIRATE SHIP, AND HE WAS TELLING ME THAT THE ONLY WAY TO WIN OUR RACE IS TO BOARD THE OTHER SHIPS... I MEAN THE OTHER CARS... AND GIVE THEM ALL A SUPLEX.
HMM. GOOD IDEA.

REALLY? OOH! THEN I SHOULD TELL YOU MY OTHER DREAM IDEAS!

I HAD THIS ONE WHERE I TURNED THE ENTIRE ROAD TO TAFFY AND THEN I ATE IT! AND THERE WAS ANOTHER DREAM WHERE ME AND A BUCKET OF ICE CREAM WERE PLAYING SOCCER AGAINST EACH OTHER. AND ANOTHER DREAM WHERE I WAS IN CLASS, BUT I DIDN'T HAVE ANY PANTS, AND ZOMBIES WERE--

NATE. I THINK WE'RE GOOD ON THE DREAMS. LET'S STICK WITH ONE PLAN AT A TIME.
SO...YOU READY?
HUH? READY FOR WHAT?

THIS!
AHHHHH!
I CALL... NOT READY!

THUMP

SUPLEX!
THORK!
SUPLEX!
SPLAMM!
SUPLEX!
FLOORP!
NRGGHH!
GRUNT!
OOOFF!
DOUBLE SUPLEX!
FLIMM!
FLAMM!

AND...SOON.
THWOOOSH!

THERE. NOW YOUR CARS ARE GONE. THE RACE IS EFFECTIVELY OVER.
THERE'S NO WAY YOU CAN MAKE IT BACK TO NEIGHBORVILLE IN TIME.

YOU'RE STRANDED!

BUT...JUST BECAUSE WE'RE NOT SUPER CRUEL...
...HERE'S A MAP ON HOW TO GET HOME.

BYE!
PEEL OUT!

BRAINS?
BRAINZZZ?
BRAINS?
BRAINS?
BRAINS?
BRAINZZZ?

?

?
STUART

BRAINS?
STUART

STUART

BRAINS?
BRAINZZZ?
STUART

BRAINS?
BRAINZZZ?
MUNCH
MUNCH
MUNCH

MEANWHILE...
WITH THE ZOMBIE CARS OUT OF COMMISSION, WE SHOULD EASILY WIN THE RACE HOME!

SO WE CAN STOP FOR A BIT, RIGHT?
The Single Best PIZZA PLACE in the WHOLE WORLD
Seriously, It's the best pizza you will ever have!!!

NO, NATE. WE CAN'T!

ZOMBOSS IS STILL IN THE RACE!
ZOMBOSS

"AND NEIGHBORVILLE CAN'T WAIT FOR US TO STOP AND EAT PIZZA."
OFFICIAL IMP WALKER
dogs love Sadie!

BUT...I'M REALLY GOOD AT EATING PIZZA!

"I'VE WON AWARDS!"
BEST EATER
MOST NAPKINS
#1 CHOMPER

I TELL YOU WHAT. IF WE WIN THE RACE BACK TO NEIGHBORVILLE, AND IF WE CAN STOP ZOMBOSS'S LATEST PLAN...

"...I'LL HAVE UNCLE DAVE COOK US ALL SOME PIZZA."

OOH! IT'S A DEAL!
LAST TIME, DAVE MADE THAT AWESOME ROBOT-SHAPED PEPPERONI AND CHOCOLATE CHIP COOKIE WITH RHUBARB PIE PIZZA!

ICE-CREAM RACER!!!
WHOOOOSH

ICE-CREAM RACER!!!
ZOOOOOOM!

HERE'S A CHICKEN!
BUH-BROCK?*
*TRANSLATION: "I'M SORRY, BUT WE CHICKENS WILL NEVER EXPLAIN WHY WE CROSSED THE ROAD. EMBRACE THE MYSTERY!"

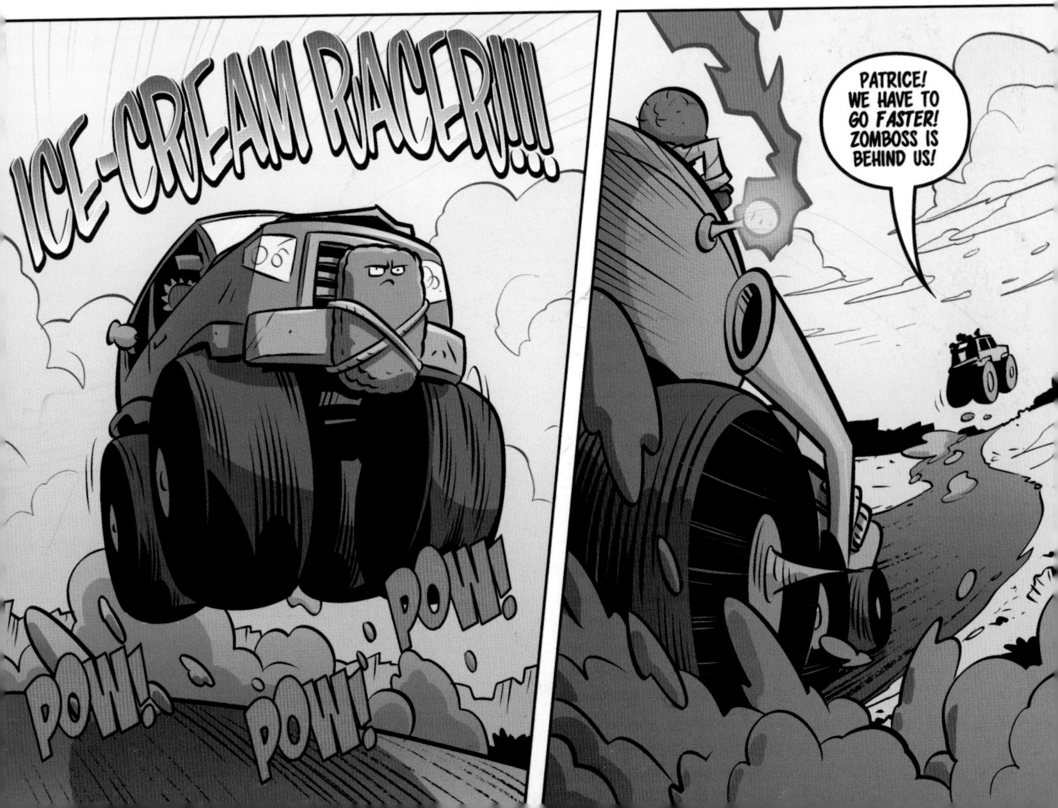
ICE-CREAM RACER!!!
POW!
POW!
POW!
PATRICE! WE HAVE TO GO FASTER! ZOMBOSS IS BEHIND US!

DEPLOY THE DISTRACTIONS!
BAMPP!

BLOOOF!!!

HA HA HA! SHIFT INTO... OVERDRIVE!
ZOMBOSS

OVER EASY DRIVE
OVERDRIVE
im so over it DRIVE

NOW, THOSE FOOLS WILL TREMBLE IN THE FACE OF THE--
FLUTTER
FLAP FLAP
FLAP FLAP
OH? WHAT'S THIS?

"...DON'T FIND THEIR WAY BACK TO THE CITY IN TIME."

SHOFFLE
SHOFFLE
SHOFFLE

ERRRRT!!!

SQUICK SQUICK SQUICK!

SQUICK!

SCREEEECH!

IS THAT A ZOMBIE?
EEK! SO SCARY!
BRAINS?
Pie Potluck Picnic

GET HIM!
SPLAPP
WHUMPFF
BLORTCH

THESE CREATURES ARE TERRIFYING, BUT...
...EASIER TO FIGHT THAN I'D THOUGHT!

MAYBE WE DIDN'T EVER NEED TO BE SCARED! MAYBE WE CAN STAND AGAINST THEM! MAYBE WE CAN FIGHT FOR OUR CITY! MAYBE WE DON'T NEED TO RUN IN HORROR!
MAYBE WE CAN STAND STRONG, AND BE BRAVE, AND WE CAN--

BUT THEN... OMINOUS MUSIC!
UH-OH.
OMINOUS MUSIC!
OH NO.

BRAINSSS!
BRAINS!
BRAINZ!
BRAINZ!
BRAINS!
BRAINS!
BRAINSSS!
BEN
YAAAAAAAHH!!!
BWAAH!
EEEK!

SLAM
THUMP!
FIDO
WHAMPH!
FOOP!
WHUMP!
CLOSED
CLUNK!
SCURRY!
WHAPP!

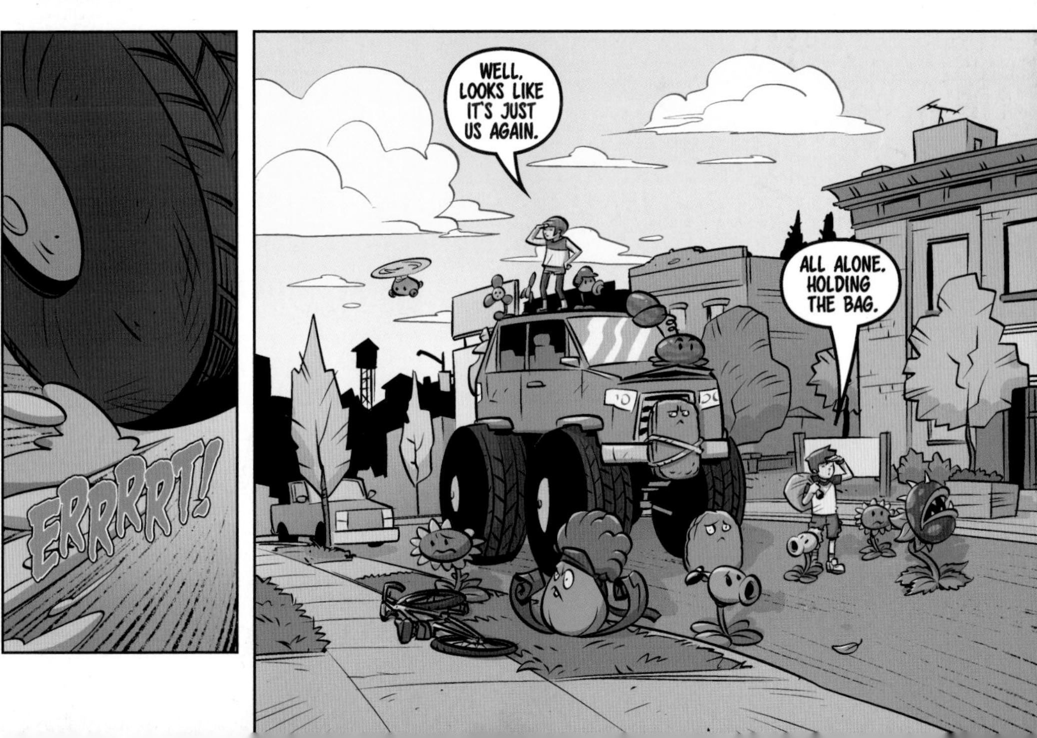
ERRRRT!
WELL, LOOKS LIKE IT'S JUST US AGAIN.
ALL ALONE. HOLDING THE BAG.

THIS BAG!
A BAG OF CANDY BRAINS!
BRAIN CANDY!*
*contains no actual brains

LISTEN UP, YOU ZOMBIES! THIS RACE ISN'T OVER!

IT'S TIME FOR A ROUND-THE-CITY DERBY!
A RACE ALL THROUGHOUT NEIGHBORVILLE!
FROZEN PARADISE
ROUND-THE-CITY DERBY!
i just wanted to say hello
AND THE WINNER GETS...

...THIS AUTOGRAPHED PICTURE OF ZOMBOSS!
UUUHHH!
GUHHH!
OOOG!

JUST KIDDING!
THE WINNER ACTUALLY GETS...
RRRIPP!

ALL THIS BRAIN CANDY!
TUMBLE TUMBLE TUMBLE

THE RACE IS ON AGAIN!

ICE-CREAM RACER!!!
ROOOARRRR!

PIGGYBACK SKATER!
ROLL
ROLL
ROLL

MR. STUBBINS AND THE WHIRLWIND SCOOTERS!
ZOOOM
WHOOOSH!
ZOOOM

THE OLD ZOMBIE NOT PARTICIPATING IN THE RACE!
ZZZ
SNORT
ZZZ

THUNDERTHUMP!
PEDAL!
PEDAL!
PEDAL!

3-2-1...GO!
WAVE!
WAVE!
WAVE!
MUNCH
MUNCH
MUNCH

VRRROOOM!

I THINK WE LOST THEM!
THUMP!

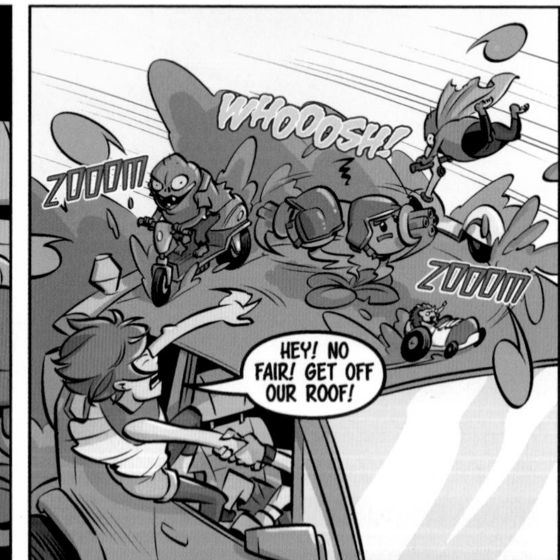
WHOOOSH!
ZOOOM
ZOOOM
HEY! NO FAIR! GET OFF OUR ROOF!

BRAAAINNSS!

POP!

THWOOOSH!
SQUICK! SQUICK! SQUIIICK!!

A PERSONAL CHALLENGE! THE GAUNTLET IS THROWN!
ARE YOU READY, MY SOON-TO-BE-DOOMED ENEMY?

YEAH. ALMOST.
ALTHOUGH MY UNDERWEAR IS RIDING UP, AND I'D APPRECIATE IT IF YOU GAVE ME A MOMENT.
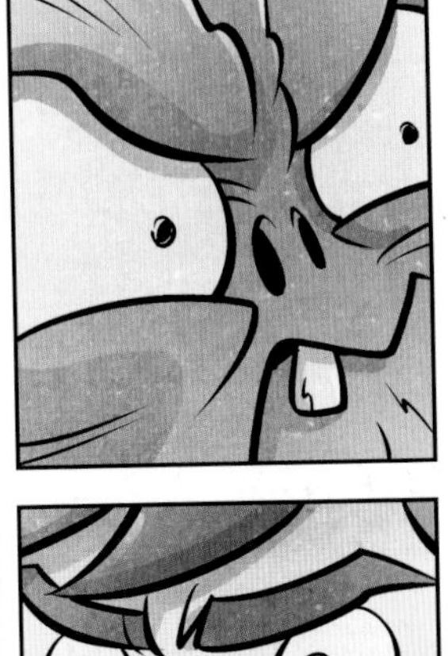

TWITCH

GO.

PUTT
PUTT
PUTT
SCREEEECH!

THIS IS ALL WORKING OUT, FRED. IF WE CAN KEEP THE ZOMBIES RACING, THEY'LL RUN OUT OF FUEL AND BECOME STRANDED...
...EASY PICKINGS FOR US IN OUR SOUPED-UP SUN-POWERED CARS.
I'M BETTING THEY'RE NOT SMART ENOUGH TO FIGURE IT OUT.

THUMP

REVERSE
REVERSE

THUMP

REVERSE
REVERSE

THUMP
I THINK WE'RE OKAY.

AND SO...
SEWER RACE!
UGH! IT SMELLS AS BAD AS A ZOMBIE IN HERE!

HALLWAY RACE!!
YOU HOOLIGANS!

VIDEO GAME RACE!
HE'S STEALING MY POPCORN!

ELEVATOR RACE!
FIFTH FLOOR! AND WE'RE *STILL* TIED!

THREE-LEGGED RACE!

DOG RACE!

PLANTS vs. ZOMBIES
RELAY RACE!

HFF!

HFF!

HUFF!
HUFF!
HUFF!

SPLAPP!

SPLURK

GO!
BRAAAAINSS!

ERRRRT!

STOP
SCREEECH

VRROOOOM!

ERRRRT!! SCREEEECH!! VROOOOMM!!
NATE, YOU DON'T ACTUALLY HAVE TO YELL OUT THE SOUND EFFECTS.

FASTER! THEY'RE CATCHING UP!

BANANAS!
WHAT? WHAT ARE YOU TALKING ABOUT?

BANANAS!
ENTIRE TRUCKLOAD OF
BANANAS ENTERPRISES

OOG!
SCREEECH!

SPLORK!

SKUFF SKUFF
SLIP!
SQUIRP

THUMP
WHUFF?

THAT HELPED!
BUT THE OTHERS ARE GETTING TOO CLOSE!

DRIVE FASTER! DRIVE FASTER!
THIS IS GETTING SCARY!

ZOOOM!
GRRR!
SCREEEECH!
RRROAAAR!
BRAINS!
BRAINS!

AND THEN...
PUTT PUTT!
?
?
POOF!
?
WRRRR

URRGH?
BRAINS?

FINALLY!
SLAPP!
THEY'RE OUT OF GAS!

CAUTIONARY NOTE: NEVER SAY THINGS LIKE THIS!

MASSIVE MUNCH MACHINE!!
HELLO.

YES. THE MASSIVE MUNCH MACHINE.
A MACHINE SO DANGEROUS, SO MASSIVE, SO INCREDIBLE, AND SO LET'S-FACE-IT-JUST-AWESOMELY-SWEET THAT IT TAKES TWO PILOTS TO CONTROL!
SQUICK! SQUICK! SQUICK!

AND IT HAS ITS OWN DISCO SOUNDTRACK!
Mr. Massive Munch Machine! You the nastiest thing I ever seen!
You Peashooters and you cute mushrooms! Just step on up and meet your doom!

PLUS IT HAS THESE BITEY TEETH PARTS.
THAT'S REALLY THE FOCAL POINT OF MY MACHINE.
YES. IT'S THESE TEETH.

FIRE! WE NEED TO TAKE THAT THING DOWN!
P-TOO P-TOO
VWEEN
THOOP
THOOP
RAWRRR!
RAWRRR!
GULP.

RETREAT!
RUN! RUN!
RUN!

SCURRY!
SCURRY!
SCURRY!

WE CAN'T STOP THIS THING! EVEN THE TRIPLE TALL-NUT WALL IS USELESS! WHAT ARE WE GOING TO DO?
SMASSSHHH!!

SNOOORRR
HUH?
Bella's Gifts
UNCLE DAVE?
CRAZY DAVE?
BRAINS?

HE'S TURNED THE DINO-PIG INTO A *ROBOT!*
INTO AN *ENGINE OF DESTRUCTION!*

AND ALSO AN *OVEN OF PIZZA!*

WE CAN'T GET IN THE MIDDLE OF THIS! WE'LL BE CRUSHED!
ALL WE CAN DO IS WATCH, AND HOPE!

AND HAVE SOME OF THIS PIZZA.
NOM! NOM!
MUNCH MUNCH

AND SET UP SOME LAWN CHAIRS...

...AND SOME PILLOWS FOR MY FEET.

I GOT THE LEMONADE!
MONSTER FIGHT LEMONADE!

OINK
OINK
KRA-
KAMM!!

CHOMP
CHOMP
CHOMP

SLAP!
OOF!
SLAP!
SLAP!
HRRF!
SLAP!
SLAP!
OWWW!
YOW!

BOOT!
POOT!

KRANNG!

BANG!
BANG!
BOOM
BOOM

KOOM!
BANG!
KRANNG!
KA-KOOM!
KRANGITTY-KRANNG!
BANGITY-BANG!

HEY! NO FAIR! THE ZOMBIES ARE ATTACKING DINO-PIG! WE HAVE TO HELP!
GIMME A SECOND. THERE'S ONE LAST SLICE...

NOW, NATE!
OOP!
AAP!
NOOOO!
FUMBLE

AND SO...
BRAINS!
BRAAINS!
BRAINZZ!
NO WAY! BAD ZOMBIE! BAD!
WHAPP!
WHAPP!

KCHAK

BLURK!
P-TOOOOEY
OOOF!

WEE! GIGGLE GIGGLE
SPASH!
SPASH!
OH, NO WAY! GROSS!

KCHUNNG
KTICK

BLOOP

PLOP

EH?

NHAMMMMMMM

SQUICK!
NO! MY BEAUTIFUL MASSIVE MUNCH MACHINE! DESTROYED!
BUT... THIS ISN'T THE END OF THIS!

OOOH! THIS IS THE END OF THIS.

AND NOW...YOU HAVE TO LEAVE NEIGHBORVILLE, FOREVER!
WHAT?
THAT'S ABSURD!

WHAT? BUT THAT WAS THE WHOLE POINT OF OUR RACE!
WHO-EVER LOSES HAS TO LEAVE NEIGHBORVILLE-- AND NEVER COME BACK!
YES, WELL, FIRST OF ALL... I NEVER KEEP MY PROMISES. EVERYBODY KNOWS THAT.

AND, SECONDLY, I DIDN'T LOSE THE RACE.

WHAT'D HE SAY?

DID SO!
DID NOT!
DID SO!
DID NOT!
DID SO!
DID NOT!
DID SO!
DID NOT!
DID SO!
DID NOT!
DID SO!
DID NOT!
DID SO!
DID NOT!
OOG NOFFLE!

HE SAID, LET'S GO TO THE REPLAY, AND THEN SOMETHING ABOUT GOLDFISH UNDERWEAR THAT I DIDN'T QUITE CATCH.

THE REPLAY!

SEE?! THERE WE ARE-- CROSSING THE FINISH LINE FIRST!
NEVER!
ZOOM IN!
FINISH LINE

It's a tie!

AND SO...LATER...
HMMM. TIME TO DEVISE A NEW PLAN. AND...I HAVE TO USE ALL OF MY BRILLIANT MIND, BECAUSE, MUCH AS I DESPISE THEM, I KNOW THAT...
...SOMEWHERE OUT THERE, CRAZY DAVE AND THOSE KIDS ARE THINKING OF A BRILLIANT PLAN OF THEIR OWN.
WHRR WHRR
WHRR

SOMEWHERE OUT THERE...
IT'S A FAN, BUT MADE OUT OF PIZZA.
TURN IT ON! TURN IT ON!
THE END!

PLANTS VS. ZOMBIES™
JACOB CHABOT 2015

BOOM BOOM MUSHROOM

Written by PAUL TOBIN
Art by JACOB CHABOT
Colors by MATT J. RAINWATER
Letters by STEVE DUTRO

Plants vs. Zombies: Boom Boom Mushroom and *Plants vs. Zombies* comic #10 cover art (previous page) by Jacob Chabot

WHYYYYY???

HOW COULD I HAVE MADE THIS MISTAKE? AS A ZOMBIE WHO CLAIMS TO BE BRILLIANT...
NiGeL

...AND I AM BRILLIANT...
NiGeL

...I CAN'T BELIEVE THAT I, DR. EDGAR ZOMBOSS, OF ALL PEOPLE, HAVE BEEN...
...PLAYING FAIR!

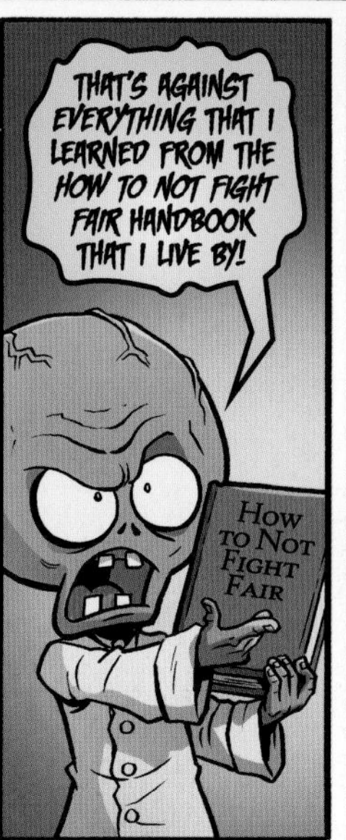
THAT'S AGAINST EVERYTHING THAT I LEARNED FROM THE HOW TO NOT FIGHT FAIR HANDBOOK THAT I LIVE BY!
HOW TO NOT FIGHT FAIR

AND THAT I ALSO WROTE.
HOW TO NOT FIGHT FAIR
BY DR. EDGAR ZOMBOSS

THINGS THAT I ESPECIALLY DO NOT LIKE...
TAP TAP TAP
THE THING IS...I KEEP STAGING MY BATTLES ABOVEGROUND, BUT THAT'S STUPID.
BECAUSE WHEN I'M ABOVEGROUND I HAVE TO DEAL WITH SUCH IRRITATING THINGS AS...
NiGeL

...SUNFLOWERS...
DUR.
DUH.
TAP TAP TAP

...PESKY CHILDREN...
BLAH BLAH
I YAM DUM!
TAP TAP

...AND MY ALLERGIES TO THIS LIST OF 74,000 DIFFERENT PLANTS.
ALLERGIC
ALLERGIC
ALLERGIC

ALSO--PEOPLE WITH HAPPY FACES!

AND CHIHUAHUAS, AND...WORST OF ALL...
TAP TAP TAP

...THE SUN!

IT'S TIME FOR A CHANGE OF TACTICS, BECAUSE BELOW GROUND IS WHERE MY KINGDOM MUST BE ESTABLISHED!
THERE... BELOW GROUND... MY RIGHTFUL SOVEREIGNTY CAN TAKE ROOT AND GROW LIKE A PLANT!
WELL, NO, NOT LIKE A PLANT...LIKE SOMETHING SIMILAR TO A PLANT, BUT VERY MUCH NOT A PLANT... BECAUSE PLANTS ARE IRRITATING.
WHAT ELSE GROWS? PANCAKES? KIND OF, I GUESS...?
AND CAKES GROW, TOO. CAKES GROW IN THE OVEN.
SO BE IT! I WILL ESTABLISH MY KINGDOM LIKE PANCAKES!
NiGel
LOOK, I'M STILL WORKING ON MY METAPHORS. THEY'RE NOT IMPORTANT.
THE IMPORTANT THING IS... CONQUEST.

CLYDE'S CAVES, CAVERNS, & CUPCAKES
TIME TO PUT MY PLAN INTO ACTION!

HERE, IN THE CAVES IN THIS VAST UNDERGROUND COMPLEX, I CAN ESTABLISH A HUGE ARMY OF ZOMBIES...
ORANGE DRINK!
...ALL WITHOUT THE IRRITATING INTERFERENCE OF PLANTS, CHIHUAHUAS, CHILDREN, OR THE SUN.

FIRST, LET'S GET RID OF ALL THESE PESTS.
EEEK! ZOMBIES!
SNIFF! SNIFF! UGH! LISTEN. COULD I INTEREST YOU FELLOWS IN SOME COMMEMORATIVE DEODORANT? SOME SOAP? SOME COLOGNE?

ATTENTION, HUMAN-PEOPLE TYPES!
EXIT TO THE LEFT IF YOU DON'T WANT YOUR BRAINS EATEN. EXIT TO THE RIGHT IF YOU WOULD LIKE TO BE A SNACK.

EXIT
EXIT
HMPH! WELL, THAT'S DISAPPOINTING.

BUT IT'S TIME FOR ME TO GET TO WORK!
AND BY THAT I MEAN--TIME TO MAKE ALL OF YOU GET TO WORK!
WE NEED TO CLEAR THESE CAVES! WE NEED ROOM! GET RID OF EVERYTHING THAT'S ALREADY HERE!

TILT-A HURL
THE TILT-A-HURL! GONE!

THE CARAVAN OF CUPCAKES! GONE!

THE WORLD'S SECOND-LARGEST GRAPE WITH A DRAWING OF A CAT ON IT!
SQUISH IT!

THE CLOSET-SIZED CAVERN OF CLOWN PAINTINGS!
NiGeL
URRGH! YEAH. THIS HAS TO GO.

I'VE CHANGED MY MIND ON THE CARAVAN OF CUPCAKES!
IT STAYS!!!

OON...
THERE. IT'S PERFECT!
ALTHOUGH THE POOL FACILITIES ARE LACKING.
AND WILL YOU ZOMBIES QUIT TRIPPING OVER MY ELECTRICAL CORDS?!?!
TRIP!
THEY HAVE TO RUN ALL THE WAY UP TO THE SURFACE WORLD AND-- SERIOUSLY--EXTENSION CORDS COST A LOT OF MONEY, SO BE CAREFUL!
TRIP!

OON...
ZOMBOSS WANTS YOU!
BRAINSSS.
BRAINS.
BRAAAINS.
BRAINZZZ.
BRAINZ
stamp 'EM OUT

ZOMBOSS WANTS YOU!
BRAINSSS.
BRAINS.
KEEP YOUR TRAP SHUT
BRAINSSS.
BRAAAINS.
BRAINZ
stamp 'EM OUT
BRAINS.
BRAAAINS.
BRAINZZZ.

ZOMBOSS WANTS YOU!
BRAINSSS.
BRAINS.
BRAINS.
BRAINS.
BRAINZZZ.
stamp 'EM OUT
DON'T STACK ZOMBIES MORE THAN TEN DEEP
NO DISCO AFTER 9 P.M.
BRAINSSS.
BRAAAINS.
BRAINS.
BRAINS.
BRAINZZZ.
IMP BARREL

BRAINS.
BRAINS.
BRAINS.
BRAINS.
BRAINSSS.
BRAAAINS.
BRAINZZZ.
BRAINSSS.
BRAINS.
BRAAAINS.
BRAINS.
BRAINS.
BRAAAINS.
BRAAAINS.
BRAAAINS.
BRAINS.
BRAAAINS.
BRAINS.
BRAINZZZ.

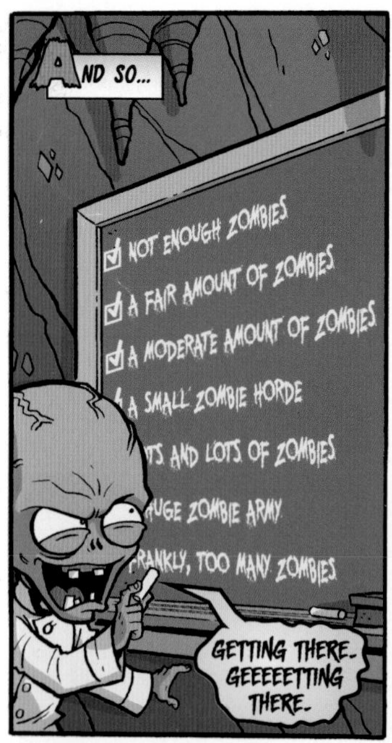
AND SO...
NOT ENOUGH ZOMBIES
A FAIR AMOUNT OF ZOMBIES
A MODERATE AMOUNT OF ZOMBIES
A SMALL ZOMBIE HORDE
TS AND LOTS OF ZOMBIES
UGE ZOMBIE ARMY
RANKLY, TOO MANY ZOMBIES
GETTING THERE. GEEEEETTING THERE.

YES...THIS UNDERGROUND COMPLEX OF CAVES IS A PERFECT FACILITY.
HERE, NOTHING CAN GO WRONG. HERE, THERE IS NOTHING TO DISTURB ME.
NIGEL

I MAY AS WELL REST FOR A MOMENT AND ENJOY SOME DELICIOUS POP SMARTS, THE BRAIN-FLAVORED TREAT!
POP SMARTS

ZZZ ZZZ ZATCH!!

FROOOOGPANTS.

-SIGH!-
WELL, BACK TO WORK.
SHAKE
SHAKE
SHAKE
YES, SOON MY ARMY WILL BE HUGE...AS MATHEMATICALLY DETERMINED BY IT BEING THREE TIMES AS BIG AS A MERE "LARGE" ARMY.
DON'T BE A SIMP. HIRE AN IMP!
AND AT THAT POINT...
...I WILL USE THESE CLEVER HYDRAULICS...

"...TO LOWER THE ENTIRE CITY OF NEIGHBORVILLE DOWN INTO MY CAVERNS, LIKE A DUMBWAITER FULL OF SWEET, DELICIOUS, BATHED-IN-DARKNESS BRAINS!"

ZOMBIE ARTIST'S CONCEPTION...
? ?
YAAAH!!
BRAINS!
HELLO, DINNER.
BRAINS!
BRAINS!
BRAINS!

MEANWHILE...
NATE? DO YOU KNOW WHERE MY UNCLE DAVE IS?
CRAZY DAVE? YOU MEAN WHERE HE IS? HOW WOULD I KNOW WHERE HE IS?
I MEAN, IT'S NOT LIKE HE AND I HAVE BEEN WORKING IN SECRET ANYWHERE! DOING SOMETHING, LIKE, YOU KNOW...
...TRYING TO MAKE MOOD ICE CREAM, ICE CREAM THAT CHANGES ACCORDING TO MOODS, LIKE A MOOD RING.

HA HA HA! THAT WOULD BE SO SILLY! WHO EVEN BROUGHT THAT UP?

NATE. IS THAT WHAT YOU AND UNCLE DAVE ARE DOING?
YES, THAT'S EXACTLY WHAT WE'RE DOING.

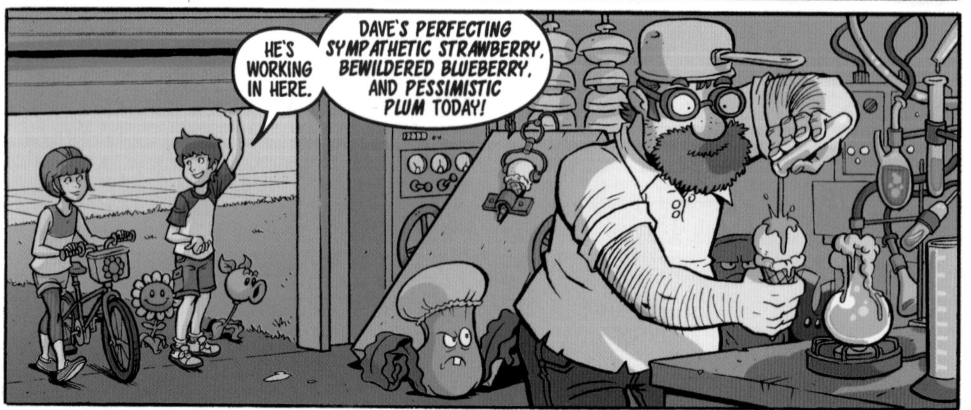
HE'S WORKING IN HERE.
DAVE'S PERFECTING SYMPATHETIC STRAWBERRY, BEWILDERED BLUEBERRY, AND PESSIMISTIC PLUM TODAY!

HMMM. DID YOU KNOW YOUR FREEZER'S BROKEN?
YOUR MOOD ICE CREAMS ARE MELTING!

HERE'S THE PROBLEM. SOMEBODY UNPLUGGED IT AND PUT IN A POWER STRIP OF THEIR OWN.
THAT'S... A LOT OF PLUGS.

WE'LL FOLLOW THESE CORDS TO SEE WHERE THEY GO AND WHO PLUGGED THEM IN.
WOW... THEY JUST KEEP GOING AND GOING AND GOING!

WELL, *THIS* LOOKS OMINOUS.
I THINK THE RESPONSIBLE THING HERE WOULD BE TO--
DANJERUSS CAVE! MONSTURRZ! NO PEZKY KIDS!

HERE WE GO!!!!
DANJERUSS CAVE! MONSTURRZ! NO PEZ KIDS!
JUST...JUST JUMP RIGHT IN, THEN... I GUESS.

OON...
THIS IS AMAZING, NATE. YOU KNOW WHAT WE'VE DISCOVERED?
YES. I DO. WE'VE DISCOVERED--

--THAT THE ZOMBIES REALLY NEED TO DO THEIR LAUNDRY.
I MEAN, C'MON, GUYS!
DO LAUNDRY ON ZATURDAY ZUNDAY MUNDAY TUEZDAY WEDNEZDAY THURZDAY

WELL, YES, THAT'S TRUE, BUT EVEN MORE IMPORTANTLY--
--WE'VE DISCOVERED ZOMBOSS'S SECRET PLAN FOR RAISING A ZOMBIE ARMY UNDERGROUND AND THEN SWALLOWING THE ENTIRE CITY OF NEIGHBORVILLE WHOLE!
WHAT? REALLY? WE HAVE?

ZOMBOSS'S SECRET PLAN FOR RAISING A ZOMBIE ARMY UNDERGROUND AND THEN SWALLOWING THE ENTIRE CITY OF NEIGHBORVILLE WHOLE!
BUY POP ZMARTZ
TAP
TAP
TAP
GENIUS
ZOMBOZZ
IMPORTANT!! DO NOT SHOW TO ANYONE WITH BRAINS!

SOON...
ZOMBOSS'S PLAN CAN'T BE ALLOWED TO SUCCEED!
BUT HOW CAN WE STOP HIM?
WELL, WHAT ABOUT AN ARMY OF REMOTE-CONTROLLED ROBOTS THAT CAN COOK PIZZAS AND FIGHT ZOMBIES AND COOK PIZZAS?
YOU SAID "COOK PIZZAS" TWICE.
YEAH. THAT'S BECAUSE THEY COOK A LOT OF PIZZAS.
WELL, I THINK WE NEED A DRAMATIC CONFRONTATION!
MUSCLE AGAINST MUSCLE! OUR ARMY AGAINST HIS!
YOU THINK WE CAN WIN AGAINST THOUSANDS OF ZOMBIES?
PROBABLY NOT, BUT THAT'S WHAT MAKES IT SO DRAMATIC!
IT DOESN'T MAKE IT ANY SMARTER.
HOW ABOUT TRAINING CATS TO FIGHT THE ZOMBIES?
TRAINING CATS?
OH, NATE, WHICH DO YOU THINK WOULD BE EASIER?
DEFEATING A THOUSAND ZOMBIES, OR TRAINING A SINGLE CAT?
WELL, WHAT ARE SOME OTHER IDEAS?

GROKKLE BLURK FLAPWAGON. PLONK GRIMFIZZLE!
UNCLE DAVE HAS AN IDEA!
WHMP
THMP
WARNING
OPEN WHENEVER
THIS SIDE UP
FUMP
???
SNIFF!
SNUFFLE!
WHAT IS *THAT*?
BLIFFLE PLOM PLOMM PLOOOOM!
DAVE SAYS HER NAME IS *TWISTER*.
SHE'S A *TRUFFLE-SNUFFLE*, A RARE GUATEMALAN... PIG-DOG? OR MAYBE DOG-PIG?
THAT'S GREAT, BUT HOW DOES TWISTER FIT IN WITH DAVE'S PLAN?
SKRITCH!
SKRATCH!

CROMTOGGLE!
UNCLE DAVE WON TWISTER IN A BARD GAME DURING A TRIP TO GUATEMALA.
A BOARD GAME?
"NO. A BARD GAME. IT'S A CONTEST WHERE BARDS SING SONGS."
GRELLBLORK SKRIP CRAM! BLUEBIRDS! FLOP-FLOGGLES!
"TOGETHER, UNCLE DAVE AND TWISTER HAD A SERIES OF AMAZING ADVENTURES.

"AND THEN, DEEP IN AN UNDERGROUND CAVERN, THEY DISCOVERED A SECRET...A RARE MUSHROOM THAT WOULD BE A GREAT HELP TO US NOW."

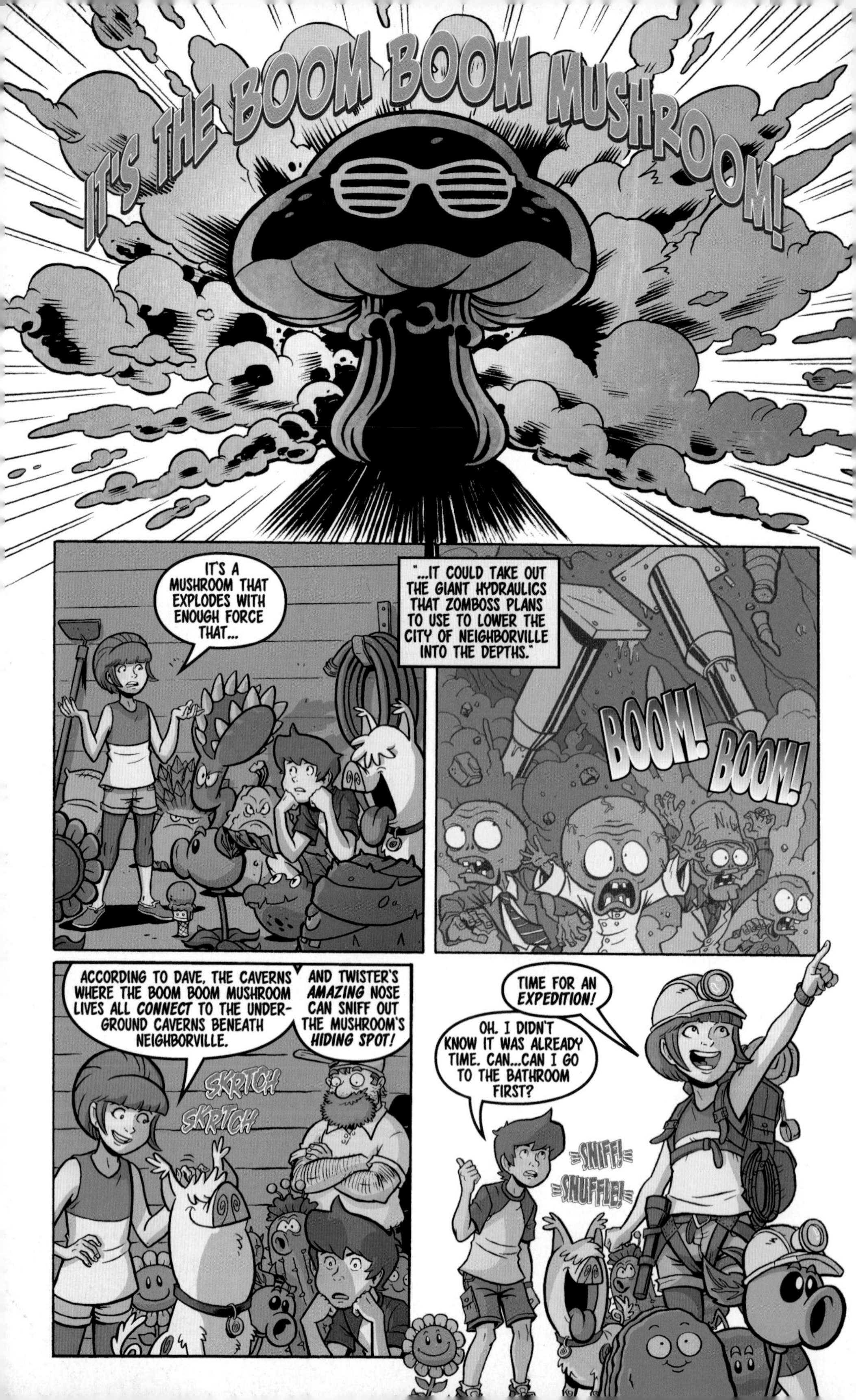
IT'S THE BOOM BOOM MUSHROOM!
IT'S A MUSHROOM THAT EXPLODES WITH ENOUGH FORCE THAT...
"...IT COULD TAKE OUT THE GIANT HYDRAULICS THAT ZOMBOSS PLANS TO USE TO LOWER THE CITY OF NEIGHBORVILLE INTO THE DEPTHS."
BOOM! BOOM!
ACCORDING TO DAVE, THE CAVERNS WHERE THE BOOM BOOM MUSHROOM LIVES ALL CONNECT TO THE UNDER-GROUND CAVERNS BENEATH NEIGHBORVILLE.
AND TWISTER'S AMAZING NOSE CAN SNIFF OUT THE MUSHROOM'S HIDING SPOT!
SKRTCH
SKRTCH
TIME FOR AN EXPEDITION!
OH. I DIDN'T KNOW IT WAS ALREADY TIME. CAN...CAN I GO TO THE BATHROOM FIRST?
SNIFF!
SNUFFLE!

MEANWHILE...
FOR THE LOVE OF BRAINS! WHO LEFT THE POPBRAIN MACHINE ON?!
POP! POP! POP! POP! POP! POP!
NIGEL BLIMPBOTTOM! IT'S YOU? I SHOULD HAVE KNOWN!
BRAINS?
POPBRAINS
THE BRAIN-FLAVORED POPCORN
NiGeL
POP! POP! POP! POP! POP!
OKAY, WE'RE GOING TO HAVE TO READJUST OUR INVASION SCHEDULE UNTIL WE CLEAN UP ALL THESE POPBRAIN SNACKS AND MAKE ROOM FOR MORE BARRACKS.
THERE.
NOT YET.
NUDGE
IN A BIT...
NOW!
HURRY UP! HURRY UP! POUR THOSE POPBRAINS SNACKS! YOU GARGANTUARS--EAT!
CHOMP!! CHOMP!! CHEW CHOMP!! CHOMP!! CHEW CHEW
MUNCH MUNCH MUNCH MUNCH

BRAINS!
BRAINZZZ!
BRAAAINS!
BRAINS!
BRAINS!
URRGH! NOW THERE'S A PROBLEM WITH THE HYDRAULICS?

TUGBOAT! DID YOU USE MY HYDRAULICS TO MAKE A JACKED-UP TUGBOAT?

TUUUGBOOOAT?

HRRR!
NUDGE
Give Me a Minute Here.
IN A BIT...
NOW!

I NEED A BREAK FROM THESE INFERIOR AND INSUFFERABLE FOOLS.
I BELIEVE I'LL RELAX WITH THE LATEST EPISODE OF ZOM-ICHI: THE NO-BRAINED SWORDSMAN.
CLICK

Zom-ichi:
The No-Brained Swordsman
Episode 105:
Still No Brains

AHHHHHHHH...

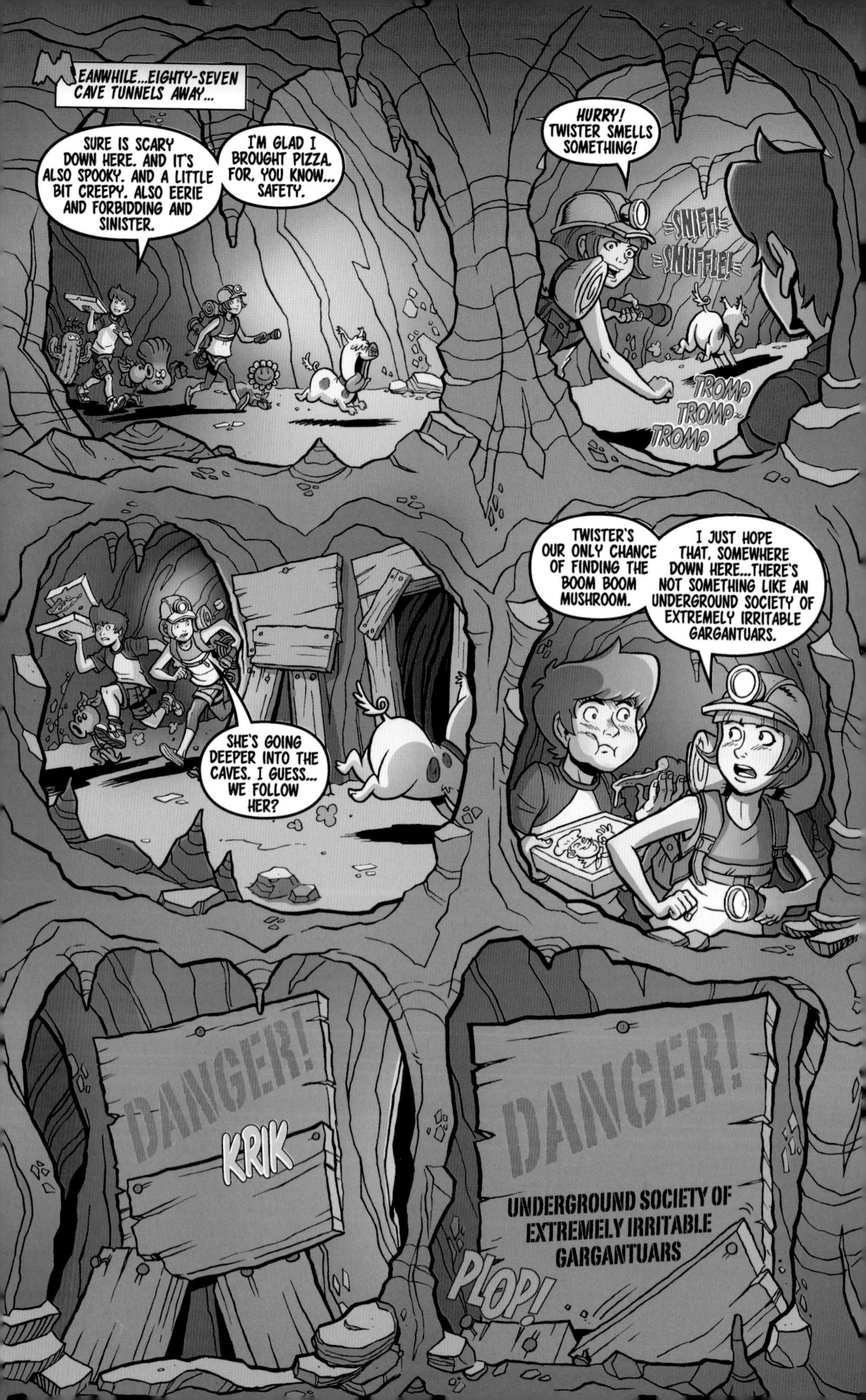
MEANWHILE...EIGHTY-SEVEN CAVE TUNNELS AWAY...
SURE IS SCARY DOWN HERE. AND IT'S ALSO SPOOKY. AND A LITTLE BIT CREEPY. ALSO EERIE AND FORBIDDING AND SINISTER.
I'M GLAD I BROUGHT PIZZA. FOR, YOU KNOW... SAFETY.
HURRY! TWISTER SMELLS SOMETHING!
SNIFF!
SNUFFLE!
TROMP
TROMP
TROMP
SHE'S GOING DEEPER INTO THE CAVES. I GUESS... WE FOLLOW HER?
TWISTER'S OUR ONLY CHANCE OF FINDING THE BOOM BOOM MUSHROOM.
I JUST HOPE THAT, SOMEWHERE DOWN HERE...THERE'S NOT SOMETHING LIKE AN UNDERGROUND SOCIETY OF EXTREMELY IRRITABLE GARGANTUARS.
DANGER!
KRIK
DANGER!
UNDERGROUND SOCIETY OF EXTREMELY IRRITABLE GARGANTUARS
PLOP!

HURRY!
THE CAVES OF MODERATELY CERTAIN DOOM & A FEW UNPLEASANT ODORS
TWISTER RUNS SO FAST, WE CAN'T GET LEFT BEHIND OR WE COULD GET LOST AND MIGHT NEVER FIND THE LEGENDARY BOOM BOOM MUSHROOM!
SAFETY FIRST
LOOKING FOR BOOM BOOM MUSHROOM? LOOKS LIKE THIS! NOT LIKE THIS!
GOOD THING CRAZY DAVE PUT ALL THESE POSTERS UP, SO WE'LL KNOW WHAT WE'RE LOOKING FOR.
WE NEED THAT MUSHROOM TO HELP US DESTROY ZOMBOSS'S LATEST PLAN.
LOOKING FOR BOOM BOOM MUSHROOM? LOOKS LIKE THIS! NOT LIKE THIS!
"SO WE KEEP FOLLOWING TWISTER--AND WE KEEP HOPING WE CAN FIND THAT MUSHROOM IN TIME!"
LOOKING FOR BOOM BOOM MUSHROOM? LOOKS LIKE THIS! NOT LIKE THIS!
LOOKING FOR BOOM BOOM MUSHROOM? LOOKS LIKE THIS! NOT LIKE THIS!
GLOINK GLOINK
GLOINK
MUNCH MUNCH MUNCH

HOURS LATER...
FOO! THIS IS HARD GOING.
GOOD THING I BROUGHT SOME WATER. AND A COMPASS. AND SOME EXTRA CLOTHES.
WHAT DID YOU BRING?
UMMM...
SNIFF!
SNOINK!
SNIFF!
COMIC BOOKS!
AND PIZZA!
AND COMIC BOOKS ABOUT PIZZA!
PIZZA PUNCH
LOST SOCK
PIZZA
CRAZY DAVE
AND THIS ROBOTIC HAT THAT CRAZY DAVE GAVE ME.
LOOK!
AT MY HAT? RIGHT?
IT'S PRETTY COOL, BECAUSE--
NO! I MEAN, LOOK!
IT'S THE BOOM BOOM MUSHROOM!

MUNCH
MUNCH
MUNCH
BUT HOW ARE WE GOING TO GET ACROSS THIS RIVER?

LOOKS LIKE WE CAN USE THAT BRIDGE, MAYBE?
DO NOT USE THIS BRIDGE

LET'S HURRY UP AND--
HUH?
AAAH!
TOSS
SKOINK!

UMPFF!
TOOT!
OOF!
WHAT JUST HAPPENED?
WAIT!
DO NOT USE THIS BRIDGE
TROMP
TROMP
TROMP

IT SAYS HERE...THAT THIS IS A PATCH OF *TOSS MOSS.*
TOSS MOSS

GAH!
APPARENTLY, IF YOU WALK ON IT, IT TOSSES YOU BACK.

AAAH!
IT SAYS HERE THAT IT'S NORMALLY VERY FRIENDLY TO ANYBODY BUT ZOMBIES, BUT...
THMMP

...I GUESS MY UNCLE DAVE ATE ALL OF THEIR SACRED BARBECUE-FLAVORED ICE CREAM...
WHOA!
TROMP
TROMP
TROMP
ROINK!

...AND NOW IT'S A BIT IRRITABLE IN GENERAL.
TROMP
TROMP
TROMP
UAAH!

ROINK!
GAH!

MEANWHILE... VERY SLIGHTLY ELSEWHERE...

NATE. IT ISN'T GOING TO WORK.

GRRR...
FWOOOP!
GAH!

HRRR...

GUHRRR...

TOSS!
YAAH!

MEANWHILE...ELSEWHERE...

FROGPANTS! ARE YOU STILL TANGLED IN THOSE CORDS?
WELL, DON'T WORRY. I'LL HELP.
STRUGGLE
STRUGGLE

TMP TMP TMP

STRUGGLE
STRUGGLE

HERE YOU ARE.
IT'S A VIDEO OF ME--STARING AT YOU--TO REMIND YOU OF ME. FOREVER.

STRUGGLE
STRUGGLE

MEANWHILE, DOWN BY THE RIVERSIDE...
DANGER!
CRAZY RIVER! NO CROSSING!
IF WE CAN'T USE THE BRIDGE, HOW ARE WE GOING TO MAKE IT ACROSS?
MAYBE TWISTER CAN FIND A WAY? DON'T PIGS HAVE REALLY AMAZING NOSES?
AMAZING PIG NOSES!!
THAT'S NOT WHAT I MEANT. I MEANT PIGS HAVE AN AMAZING SENSE OF SMELL.
AND I KNOW TWISTER'S NOT REALLY A PIG, BUT IF SHE'S SO GOOD AT SMELLING OUT THE BOOM BOOM MUSHROOM, THEN...
...MAYBE SHE CAN FIND US... SOMETHING TO HELP US ACROSS THE RIVER?
HMM...IT'S POSSIBLE.
TOOT!
LET'S SEARCH AROUND HERE.
SNIFF! SNIFF!
SNIFF! SNIFF!
NOM! NOM!
SHE FOUND SOMETHING! LET'S DIG OVER THERE!
SNIFF! SNIFF!

DIG
LOOK! IT'S--
DIG
DIG
DIG
DIG
AN IRON STATUE OF A THREE-HEADED DUCK...?
AND SEVENTY-FIVE CRAZY DAVE DISCO CHAMPION SHIRTS, AND...
DISCO CHAMPION
...THE LEGENDARY HUGE RUBBER BAND...
"...THE VERY ONE THAT CAPTAIN CHESTBEARD USED TO USE TO KEEP HIS CHEST BEARD IN A PONYTAIL."
DISCO CHAMPION
ALL PIRATE COMICS
WET CAT SAGA
PIZZA PUNCH
PIZZA NO MORE?
PLUSH CHAIR
URGH! IT'S ALL GREASY!
EWWW. BUT, AH...NATE? USING THESE THREE THINGS, I THINK WE CAN MAKE IT ACROSS THE RIVER!

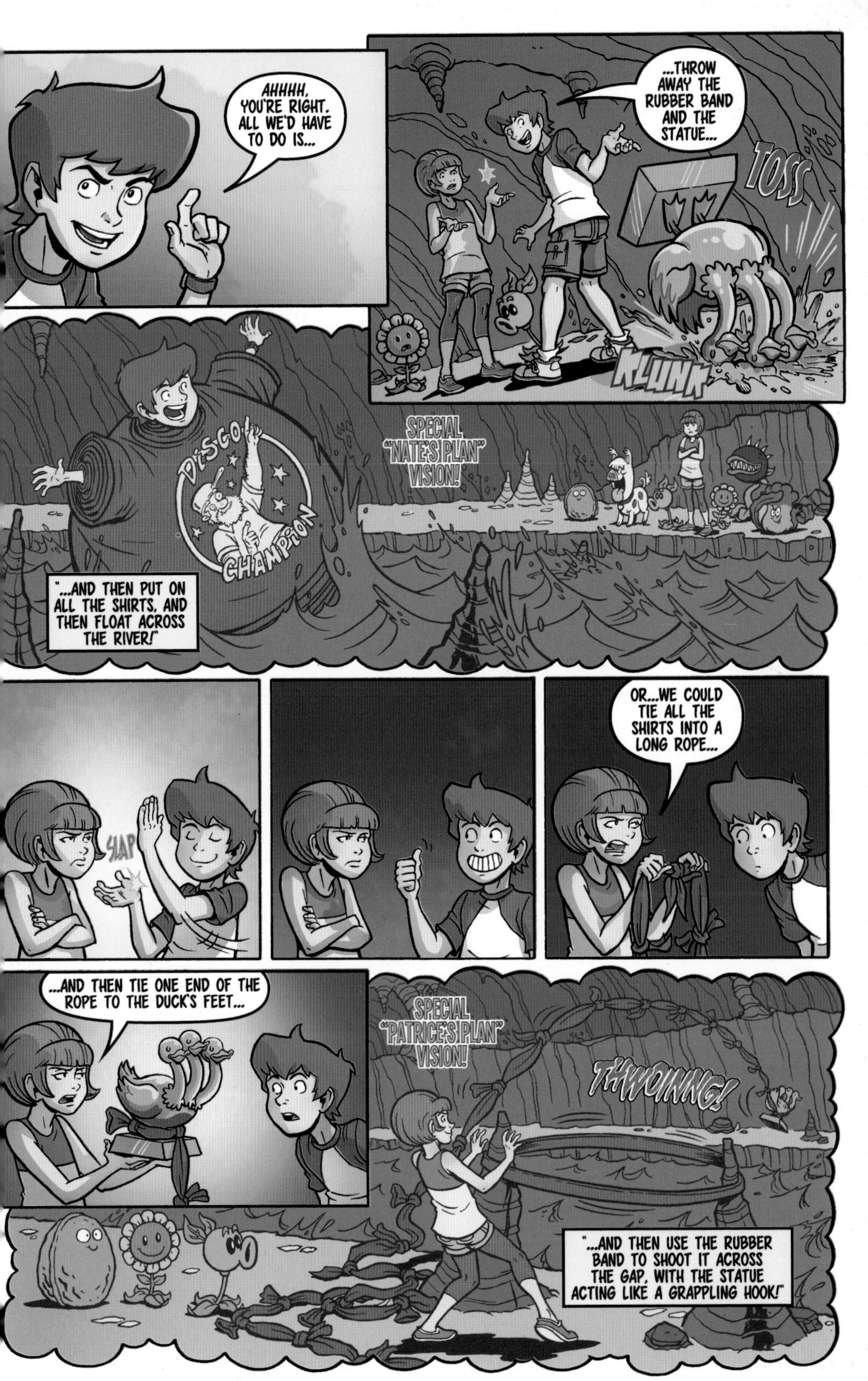
AHHHH, YOU'RE RIGHT. ALL WE'D HAVE TO DO IS...
...THROW AWAY THE RUBBER BAND AND THE STATUE...
TOSS
KLUNK
SPECIAL "NATE'S PLAN" VISION!
DISCO CHAMPION
"...AND THEN PUT ON ALL THE SHIRTS, AND THEN FLOAT ACROSS THE RIVER!"
SLAP
OR...WE COULD TIE ALL THE SHIRTS INTO A LONG ROPE...
...AND THEN TIE ONE END OF THE ROPE TO THE DUCK'S FEET...
SPECIAL "PATRICE'S PLAN" VISION!
THWOINNG!
"...AND THEN USE THE RUBBER BAND TO SHOOT IT ACROSS THE GAP, WITH THE STATUE ACTING LIKE A GRAPPLING HOOK!"

OKAY.
YOUR PLAN WINS.
WHATEVER.

AND SO, SOON...
URRF! ARRGH!
OH, NO! MY PIZZA!

SHFF
SHFF
SHFF
DINK
DINK
DOOBLE DOOBLE

HOPEFULLY WE CAN STILL CATCH UP WITH THAT MUSHROOM!
PIGGYBACK RIDE!!

MEANWHILE...
WE MARCH!
IT'S TIME TO TAKE OUR POSITIONS--AND THEN LOWER THE ENTIRE CITY OF NEIGHBORVILLE INTO OUR GRASP!
MARCH, MY ZOMBIES! MARCH!
EHHH?
WHO LEFT ALL THIS DIRTY LAUNDRY IN THE WAY?
WE SERIOUSLY NEED TO DO SOME LAUNDRY FIRST.
TOSS
HMPH!
25¢
WHO HAS SOME QUARTERS?
ANYONE?
QUARTERS?

FIFTY-TWO CAVERN TUNNELS AND ONE CONVENIENCE STORE LATER...
SLOW DOWN, NATE!
TWISTER SAYS TO GO THIS WAY!
SKROINK!
TROMP
TROMP
WE SHOULD HAVE TWISTER ON A LEASH! SHE DOESN'T UNDER-STAND DANGER.
HUH? WHAT DO YOU MEAN?
KROOOOOM!
DANGER! ROCK FALLS!
WHUDD!
TROMP
TROMP
TROMP
DANGER! BOTTOMLESS PITS!
TROMP
TROMP
TROMP
SPROING
ZIP
POP!
ZIP
DANGER! TOASTERS!
POP!
TROMP
TROMP
HMM, I SEE WHAT YOU MEAN, BUT WE'RE THROUGH THE WORST OF IT NOW. I DON'T THINK WE'RE IN ANY...

...DANGER.
Welcome to
Dangerously Irritable
Gargantuar City
Population:
So very very many
Gargantuars

WAVE
WAVE

ANGER MANAGEMENT
CLUBS FOR SMASHING!!
ER...

ER...

ANGER MANAGEMENT
CLUBS FOR SMASHING!!
ER...

ANGER MANAGEMENT
CLUBS FOR SMASHING!!

ON THE COUNT OF ONE...WE RUN!
THOOM!
THOOM!
THOOM!

ONE!

FLOAT
FLOAT
FLOAT

ZIP!
FSH
POP!
POP!
SPROING

GLARE!
GLARE!
GLARE!

STRUGGLE
STRUGGLE

FLOAT
FLOAT
FLOAT
MUNCH
MUNCH
MUNCH

FLOAT
FLOAT
OH, YES. VERY NICE.

BRAINS. BRAAAAINS!
HUH? THOSE KIDS? EVEN HERE IN MY UNDERGROUND LAIR?
I'LL TAKE CARE OF THIS! I'LL SEND MY VERY BEST ZOMBIE!

HMM...

NiGEL
HMM...HMM... HMM...

NiGEL
HMM...

MR. STUBBINS!
I HAVE A JOB FOR YOU!

HERE, LET ME WHISPER THIS EVIL PLAN INTO YOUR EAR.

WHISPER WHISPER WHISPER WHISPER WHISPER WHISPER WHISPER WHISPER WHISPER WHISPER WHISPER WHISPER WHISPER WHISPER

HA!
KICK!
OUCH!
I THINK I JUST DENTED MY TOES!
NATE! WE NEED A PLAN OF RUNNING!
YOINK!
KRAKKA-KOOM!
WE NEED A PLAN OF ACTION! EVERYONE--CONCENTRATE AN ATTACK ON THAT ONE!
WE NEED TO LESSEN THEIR NUMBERS!
THOOM
FAP!
FAP!
HRR!
GRR!
GRAH!
GREASY RUBBER BAND ATTACK!
SNAP!

SKOINNK!
PORK!
ULTIMATE PIG DROP!
UUUHHRR...
UHHHHHHH...
HA! WE GOT HIM!
FWOMMPP!
OUCH.
GREAT WORK, EVERYONE! WE TOOK ONE DOWN!
NOW ALL WE HAVE LEFT ARE...

...INFINITE GARGANTUARS.
OKAY, WE'RE IN REAL TROUBLE HERE! IF ONLY SOMEBODY WOULD COME OUT OF THE BLUE AND SAVE US!
YEAH! IF ONLY!

SHUFF!

AH...
WHO'S THAT?

OH, IT'S JUST OLD PHIL, THE COWBOY ZOMBIE.
BRAINSSS.
Lasso!
SPOORK!
UH-OH!
GRAB!

FEEL...MY... WRATH!
PUNCH
PUNCH
PUNCH
THUMP
PUNCH
THUMP
PUNCH
PUNCH
PUNCH
THUMP
WHUMP!
WHUMP!

SCUFF!

WAIT! WHO'S THAT?
ERRRG?
?!

WHAP WHAP
WHAP

ZROOOM

CHARGE!

POP!
Pop Smarts
TERROR
FLAVORED
DING!

RETREAT!

BRAINSSS...

STRUGGLE
STRUGGLE

BRIFF CLOG PANDLE DROP?
PAINT
PAINT
PAINT

ZOOOM

LEGENDARY FOUNTAIN OF YOUTH
CHEESY FOUNTAIN OF FONDUE
PUTT PUTT PUTT
CHEESY FOUNTAIN OF FONDUE
RRRREWW
SQUICK!
SOUVENIR POSTCARDS
SOUVENIR POSTCARDS
SQUICK!
SKREE!
SPOOSH
SPOOSH
SPOOSH
SQUICK!
SOON...
FWOOP!
FWOOP!
FWOOP!
FWOOP!
FOUNTAIN OF LOST SOCKS
ZROOOM
FWOOP!
FWOOP!
FWOOP!
FWOOP!
FOUNTAIN OF LOST SOCKS
FWOOP!
FWOOP!
FWOOP!
FWOOP!
VRRRTT!

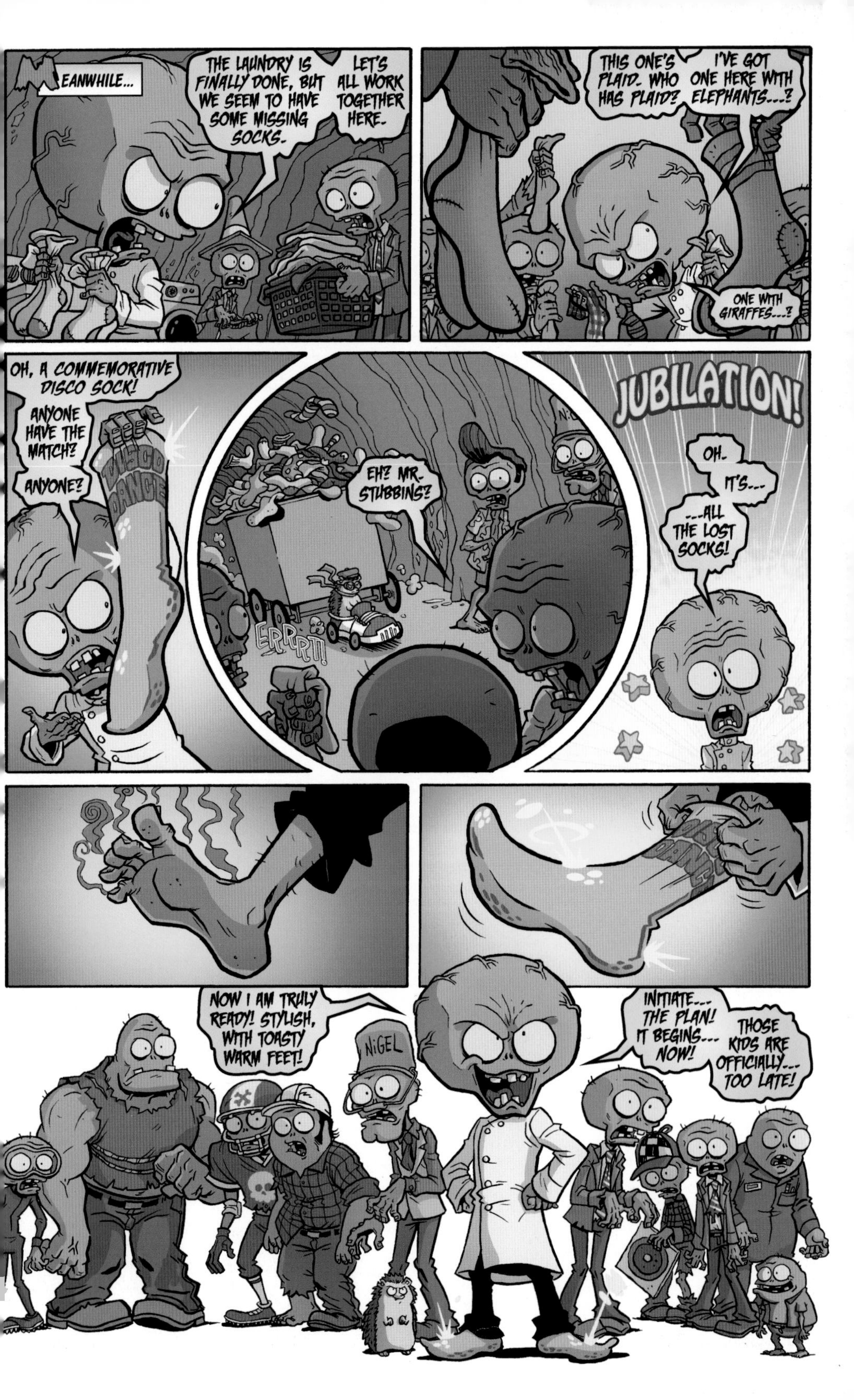
MEANWHILE...
THE LAUNDRY IS FINALLY DONE, BUT WE SEEM TO HAVE SOME MISSING SOCKS.
LET'S ALL WORK TOGETHER HERE.
THIS ONE'S PLAID. WHO HAS PLAID?
I'VE GOT ONE HERE WITH ELEPHANTS...?
ONE WITH GIRAFFES...?
OH, A COMMEMORATIVE DISCO SOCK!
ANYONE HAVE THE MATCH?
ANYONE?
DISCO DANCE
EH? MR. STUBBINS?
ERRRT!
JUBILATION!
OH.
IT'S...
...ALL THE LOST SOCKS!
NOW I AM TRULY READY! STYLISH, WITH TOASTY WARM FEET!
NIGEL
INITIATE... THE PLAN! IT BEGINS... NOW!
THOSE KIDS ARE OFFICIALLY... TOO LATE!

MEANWHILE, A FEW TUNNELS AWAY...
FIGHTING THESE ZOMBIES ISN'T WORKING! LET'S TRY RUNNING AND SCREAMING!
I'M ON IT!
BUT THEN...
WAIT! THERE! LOOK! THAT MYSTERIOUS FIGURE AGAIN!
IF WE CAN'T STOP THESE GUYS, MAYBE WE CAN GET HELP FROM...

"...THAT MUSHROOM?"

OH, GOSH! IT'S HERE!
IT'S HERE!

THE LEGENDARY BOOM BOOM MUSHROOM HAS BEEN FOUND!
CLAP CLAP
CLAP CLAP
CLAP CLAP
CLAP CLAP
CLAP CLAP
CLAP
CLAP
RUMMMBLE
FOOT!
UH-OH. SOUNDS LIKE HE'S READY TO GO BOOM-BOOM!
WE BETTER LET HIM DO HIS THING!
RUMBLE

RUMBLE
RUMBLE
RUMBLE
RUMBLE
RUMBLE
RUMBLE
BOOM BOOM

BOOM!
BOOM!

HOFF!
HOFF!

BRAINS?

BRAINS?
BRAINS?
BRAINS?

HURRY! RUN BEFORE THEY RECOVER!
BOOM BOOM--RIDE ON TWISTER!

OR...MY HEAD.
YOU COULD JUST RIDE ON THE TOP OF MY HEAD.
NATE! WE'RE RUNNING OUT OF TIME!
WE HAVE TO STOP ZOMBOSS!
ZOMBOSS PLANS TO LOWER THE ENTIRE CITY OF NEIGHBORVILLE INTO THE CAVES... AND INTO HIS ARMY!
YOU AND THE BOOM BOOM MUSHROOM NEED TO REACH THAT HYDRAULIC ELEVATOR BEFORE THAT HAPPENS, AND THEN...
...YOU BLOW IT UP!
BOOM
BOOM
WE RIDE!
RUN, TWISTER!
RUN LIKE THE TWISTED WIND!

MEANWHILE...
...CRAZY DAVE BEGINS AN IMPORTANT CAVE PAINTING!

FLOMTOGGLE!

AND THEN, SOME CAVE KARAOKE.
FRONG GRIBBLE! GIRGGLE MOO! IT'S LOOOOVE!

AND ALSO SOME CAVE INTERPRETIVE DANCE.
SKRIFF

SCRUMPFF
SCRUMPFF
SHIFF

SLIIIIIDE

OKAY, GANG. WHILE *NATE* BLOWS UP THAT HUGE HYDRAULIC ELEVATOR, *WE* HAVE TO PROTECT HIM, AND THAT MEANS...

NO...NOT BLANKETS AND PILLOWS.
IT MEANS...

...WE HAVE TO FIGHT *THOSE THINGS!*

DANG THE TORPEDOES!
FULL SPEED AHEAD!
DON'T FIRE UNTIL YOU SEE THE DUMBS OF THEIR BRAINS!

FOOSH
PFOOT!
PFOOT!
KEEP FIRING!
I'M GOING TO KEEP UNPLUGGING THESE ELECTRICAL CORDS!
MAYBE THAT WILL DO SOME GOOD!

STRUGGLE
STRUGGLE

AND SO...
WHY ISN'T MY TOASTER WORKING? HOW CAN I TOAST MY POP SMARTS?
NOBODY BETTER HAVE UNPLUGGED MY TOASTER!
AND ALSO...
KEEP MOVING!
MOVING TARGETS, EVERYONE! OUR ADVANTAGE OVER THE ZOMBIES IS SPEED!
BONK
THMP
POOM
SPEED... AND BRAINS!
BRAINS?
NO...I JUST MEANT, WE HAVE THE ADVANTAGE BECAUSE WE'RE SMARTER THAN YOU.

BRAINS?
NO, SERIOUSLY, WE ARE A LOT SMARTER THAN YOU.

FIGHT!
THAP
WHK
WACK
WHK
THOOP
PFOOT!
PFOOT!
WHY ARE THESE GUYS STILL HERE, ANYWAY? I THOUGHT I HEARD ZOMBOSS SAY HE WAS READY TO BEGIN.
I WONDER WHAT'S HOLDING UP HIS REVERSE INVASION ATTEMPT...

MEANWHILE...
YESSSS. THESE SOCKS.

SOOO GOOD TO HAVE THESE SOCKS.

MAYBE I SHOULD BE A SOCK MODEL?

ELSEWHERE, MORE EXCITEMENT...

MAN, YOU'RE MESSED UP IN THERE.

STRUGGLE
STRUGGLE

MY PIZZA SLICES! I SEE THEM IN THE RIVER!
PIZZA

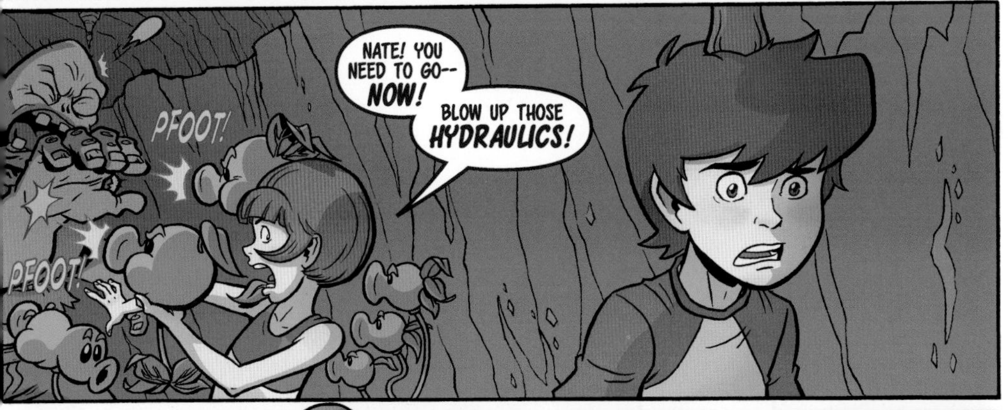
PFOOT!
PFOOT!
NATE! YOU NEED TO GO-- NOW!
BLOW UP THOSE HYDRAULICS!

PATRICE! YOU DON'T UNDERSTAND!

PEPPERONI!

TOO LATE, YOU LESSER-BUT-ADMITTEDLY-SOMEWHAT-BETTER-SMELLING FOOLS!
THOUGH YOU'VE FOLLOWED ME INTO THESE CAVERNS...
NiGEL
VRUMMM!
...AND THOUGH YOU'VE FOUND A PESKY NEW PLANT, IT MATTERS NOT! BECAUSE...
...YOU'VE LOST!
MY UNDER-GROUND REVERSE INVASION PLAN IS... COMPLETE!
LET THE HYDRAULICS BEGIN!
ZZZZ-ZZZZ-
ZOOOM
MY ARMY IS ASSEMBLED AND IT'S TIME TO...
...LOWER THE CITY!
GRIND GRIND GRIND
PAT PAT PAT
RUN RUN RUN

GRIND GRIND
WHRRRR
WHRRRR

KRRITCH
?

GRIND
WAIT. WHY ARE WE GOING ---UP?
THE CITY IS SUPPOSED TO BE COMING DOWN, TO US!
GRIND
WHRRRR
WHRRRR

WHY ARE WE---

---GOING UP INTO THE STREET---?
?

GAHHH! THE SUN!

GAHHH! CHIHUAHUA!
BARK! BARK!
BARK! BARK!

GAHHH! MY ALLERGIES!
IS MY FACE BREAKING OUT? IS ANYTHING MARRING MY BEAUTIFUL SKIN?

AT LEAST THE STREETS ARE QUIET...
NO PESKY CHILDREN OR IRRITATING CROWDS THAT--
NIGEL

NIGEL
RUMBLE RUMBLE

NIGEL
RUMBLE RUMBLE RUMBLE RUMBLE RUMBLE RUMBLE

RUMMMBLE RUMBLE RUMBLE
Welcome to Neighborville's Annual
JOGGING OF THE BULLS
(please make sure all bulls jog at a reasonable rate)
UH-OH...
RUMBLE RUMBLE

Welcome to Neighborville's Annual
JOGGING OF THE BULLS
(please make sure all bulls jog at a reasonable rate)
RUMBLE
RUMBLE
N·GEL
14
RUMBLE
GAHHH!
RUMBLE
RUMBLE RUMBLE
RUMBLE RUMBLE
RUMBLE
GAHHH!
RUMBLE
RUMBLE
RUMBLE RUMBLE
STRUGGLE
STRUGGLE

WELL, THAT WAS TERRIBLE.
BUT NOW, I BELIEVE IT'S TIME FOR THE COLOSSAL INTELLECT OF DR. EDGAR ZOMBOSS TO REIGN SUPREME!
WE WILL TAKE ADVANTAGE OF OUR SURPRISE APPEARANCE IN THIS CITY TO--

FUPP!

THOPP

OWWW...
THROB THROB

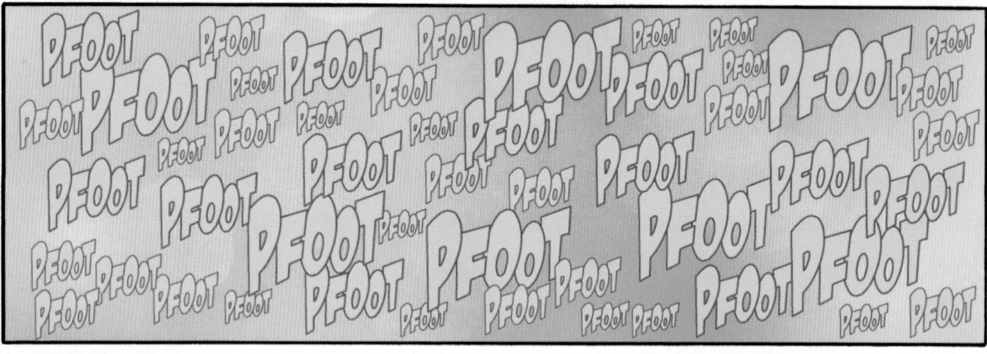
PFOOT PFOOT

SO...THEY DARE?
THEY DARE?!?!
WELL THEN, HEED ME, MY ZOMBIE HORDE, FOR AT THIS MOMENT, MY MASSIVE INTELLECT SAYS...

...RUN!

OKAY, YOU CAN'T REALLY RUN. WELL, THEN... SHUFFLE! SHUFFLE AT FULL SPEED!
THAP
SHUFFLE
SHUFFLE
SHUFFLE

SHUFFLE
SHUFFLE
SHUFFLE

NIGEL
SHUFFLE
SHUFFLE
SHUFFLE
SHUFFLE

RUN THIS WAY!!!
RUMBLE
RUMBLE
RUMBLE

SO...WERE YOU THE ONE RESPONSIBLE FOR THE WAY THAT ELEVATOR BACKFIRED ON THEM?
KIND OF.
"I HAPPENED TO NOTICE THE PLAN ON DAVE'S CAVE PAINTING.
"AND THEN ALL I HAD TO DO WAS REWIRE THE ELECTRONICS SO THAT IT WOULD WORK IN REVERSE."

AND...YOU DID THAT?
NO. I ASKED TWISTER FOR HELP.
FROOT!

WELL, GOOD JOB ANYWAY. IT LOOKS LIKE...
SMACK

"...ZOMBOSS LOSES AGAIN.

"BUT AT LEAST HE KNOWS...

"...WHERE ALL THOSE LOST SOCKS WENT."
THE END.

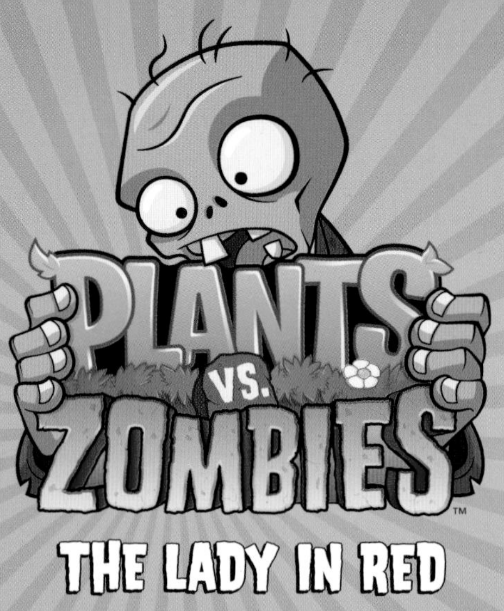

THE LADY IN RED

Written by PAUL TOBIN
Art by BRIAN CHURILLA
Letters by STEVE DUTRO

Celebrating 15 Years
FREE COMIC BOOK DAY

The Free Comic Book Day story that introduced Nate's Shroompoo Shampoo!

HE LADY IN RED
It was a cruel and vicious case, the kind that can ruin a man.
The kind of story that makes you stare deep into your soul and wonder where everything's gone wrong.
SHROOMPOO... FOR THAT CLEAN-SMELLING MUSHROOM SCENT!
It was the kind of case where you always keep your squirt gun close.

The kind of case that always seems to start with a lady in red knocking on my office door.
KNOCK KNOCK
NATE! YOU IN THERE?

Yeah. I was in there. I was also in trouble, and I knew it. The girl's name was Patrice, and everything about her was trouble. She looked like trouble. Smelled like trouble.
KNOCK KNOCK KNOCK
Meanwhile, I looked like I would need a shave in five or six years, and I smelled like mushrooms because of my favorite shampoo.

Ten minutes later, we were on the streets. There was no time for small talk, or sweet talk, or for any talk at all except making a call to the boys.

They arrived in minutes. I figured I could use their muscle, because the case already smelled bad, and so did I, because I'd forgotten to do my laundry.

The girl told me that a member of the Sunshine family--just a little tot--had been kidnapped.
A zombie had her. Not good news. The zombies are tough customers, and they smell worse than my laundry, which I believe I've mentioned wasn't so rosy.
SNIFF
SNIFF

We hadn't gone far before my keen senses alerted me to the fact that we were being followed. In my job, you notice the little things.

The big mug had a note. He handed it to me with fear in his eyes, likely terrified of my rough-and-tumble reputation.

The note said that Doc Zomboss had the baby. Even for a fighter like me, that was bad news. The worst.
BRAAAAINS

Doc Zomboss runs the city's underworld. He's a dangerous customer, with an army under his command--an army that it now looked like I was going to have to fight.
I gave a huge sigh and made sure my water pistol was full.

NO MATTER HOW TERRIBLE THE DANGER, NO MATTER WHAT I WAS UP AGAINST, THERE WAS NOTHING TO DO BUT GO FULL THROTTLE!
I WAS IN THE THICK OF IT NOW, AND THERE WAS NO BACKING OUT. I KNEW THAT LADY IN RED WAS TROUBLE THE SECOND SHE KNOCKED ON MY DOOR.
NATE, WHAT ARE YOU TALKING ABOUT?

Zomboss wanted a meet. Down by the public pool. It was probably a trap but what's a guy to do? You just buckle down, keep your head straight, and walk in with your chin up.
AAAAH!
PUBLIC POOL
COME ON, NATE!

The kid was in the pool. No water. Not a drop. Just the kid.

I was reaching for him when it all went wrong.
UH, NATE...?

Zomboss...and his gang of uglies. It was too bad the pool was dry, because they all could have used a bath.

Zomboss started ranting, the way these types do. They all have egos the size of a tree...and mercy the size of a twig.
HA! YOU FELL FOR MY TRAP! AND I'VE SPENT MONTHS ON THIS AMAZING DEVICE, WHICH CAN TRIGGER AN AMAZING VARIETY OF TRULY NEFARIOUS ACTIONS, LIKE...

...SENDING YOU BACK IN TIME, OR MAKING YOU BURP UNCONTROLL-ABLY, OR TURNING YOUR UNDERWEAR INSIDE OUT, OR SHRINKING YOU TO THE SIZE OF AN ANT, OR MAKING YOU ALLERGIC TO SUNSHINE, OR...
I knew I'd only have one shot at this--

--and I took it.
SPLLURRT!!

CLORK!
FZZZT!

SPIT!
FIZZLE!

OH, YOU'VE GOT TO BE KIDDING.

I'M GOING HOME.
TOSS!

Ten minutes later, we were at my favorite watering hole, and I was buying a round for the house. Mine was two scoops, the way I like it.
I kept it close, too. I didn't like the way the lady in red was looking at my ice cream.

And I knew that girl was trouble.
THE END.

BONUS STORIES

CHESTBEARD'S REVENGE!

Written by PAUL TOBIN
Art by KARIM FRIHA
Letters by STEVE DUTRO

A DAY IN THE LIFE(ISH) OF A ZOMBIE!

Written by PAUL TOBIN
Art by NNEKA MYERS
Letters by STEVE DUTRO

THE ZOMBIE THAT WAS AFRAID OF THE DARK

Written by PAUL TOBIN
Art by NNEKA MYERS
Letters by STEVE DUTRO

KNOW YOUR ZOMBIE HOLIDAYS!

Written by PAUL TOBIN
Art by BRIAN CHURILLA
Letters by STEVE DUTRO

THE DEVELOPMENT OF THE BALLOON ZOMBIE

Written by PAUL TOBIN
Art by BRIAN CHURILLA
Letters by STEVE DUTRO

NOISE FROM THE BOYS

Written by PAUL TOBIN
Art bwwy CAT FARRIS
Letters by STEVE DUTRO

THE COUPON

Written by PAUL TOBIN
Art by MATT J. RAINWATER
Letters by STEVE DUTRO

THE ADVENTURES OF SHERLOCK BRAINS: THE ZOMBIE WORLD'S FOREMOST CONSULTING DETECTIVE

Written by PAUL TOBIN
Art by RACHEL DOWNING
Letters by STEVE DUTRO

THE ADVENTURES OF SHERLOCK BRAINS: THE CASE OF THE PURLOINED POP SMARTS!

Written by PAUL TOBIN
Art by CHRIS SHERIDAN
Letters by STEVE DUTRO

TOASTED

Written by PAUL TOBIN
Art by JEREMY VANHOOZER
Letters by STEVE DUTRO

THE SCENIC VIEW

Written by PAUL TOBIN
Art by JEREMY VANHOOZER
Letters by STEVE DUTRO

ICE SCREAM

Written by PAUL TOBIN
Art by JEREMY VANHOOZER
Letters by STEVE DUTRO

Chestbeard's Revenge!
Story by Paul Tobin
Art by Karim Friha
Letters by Steve Dutro
SUN'S GOING DOWN.
A-YEP.
FOG'S ROLLING IN.
A-YEP.
LOOKS LIKE A TIDAL WAVE'S FLOODING THE TOWN.
A-YEP.
PIRATE SHIP.
LOOKS TO BE. A-YEP.

AAAH! HA HA HA!
IT'S I, CHESTBEARD!
I'VE BRAVED THE SEAS OF TIME ITSELF TO GAIN MY REVENGE ON THE PLANTS AND ZOMBIES WHO STOLE MY TREASURE!
SQUAWWK! IT HAPPENED IN PLANTS VS. ZOMBIES: TIMEPOCALYPSE!
AND NOW, NEIGHBORVILLE--FEAR ME! FEAR THE SCARIEST AND HAIRIEST PIRATE WHO'S EVER SAILED THE SEAS!
OR IN THIS CASE--THE STREETS, WHICH I HAVE FLOODED SO THAT I MAY DO PIRATE THINGS!

Pirate things!
LOOT THAT STORE, MEN! WE NEED GUMBALLS!
GUMBALLS
We have so many gumballs
Seriously, just gumballs

Pirate things!
BURY THE TREASURE CHEST!
DIG DIG DIG
YOU'RE RUINING MY CARPET!

Pirate things!
CHESTBEARD, LOOK AT ME!
LOOK AT ME!
HEY! HEY! LOOK AT ME!
I SEE YOU, TIMMY! I'M WATCHING!

HARR HARR HARR!
YE THINK PLANTS CAN STOP ME?
NAY! NAY! A THOUSAND TIMES NAY!
THAT WAS ONLY THREE NAYS, BOSS.
I THINK THE REST OF THEM ARE ASSUMED, DIRK.
HARR! YE THINK ZOMBIES CAN STOP ME?
NAY! NAY! THREE TIMES NAY!
THAT'S BETTER.
I CAN'T BELIEVE YOU'RE MAKING AN ISSUE OF THIS.
NEIGHBORVILLE IS MINE!
ADMITTEDLY A BIT SOGGY, BUT MINE!
TIME TO CELEBRATE!
WHO'S FOR A MANDATORY HUG? GET IN LINE!
OH, I DON'T LIKE THIS PART.
CAN I BE EXCUSED? I HAVE A DENTAL APPOINTMENT.
WAIT! WHAT'S THAT?
SOMEBODY ALONE! IN A BOAT!
IS IT SOME HERO? NEIGHBORVILLE'S CHAMPION OF JUSTICE?

NOPE. IT'S JUST A CARTON OF ORANGE JUICE.
AAAAAHHH! ROBOT ORANGE JUICE!
leap
HE'S...
HE'S SHAVING ME CHEST, LADS!
I'M UNDONE.
MY STRENGTH--VANISHED. MY SKIN--PINK.
I CAN'T... I CAN'T LET PEOPLE SEE ME LIKE THIS. -SOB!-
WE'RE OUTTA HERE.
And so ends...the Legend of the Robot Orange Juice!

Story by **Paul Tobin** • Art by **Nneka Myers** • Letters by **Steve Dutro**

A Day in the Life(ish) of a Zombie!

Zombie Fun Page!

Let's take a look at the exciting, thrill-a-minute daily life(ish) of a zombie!

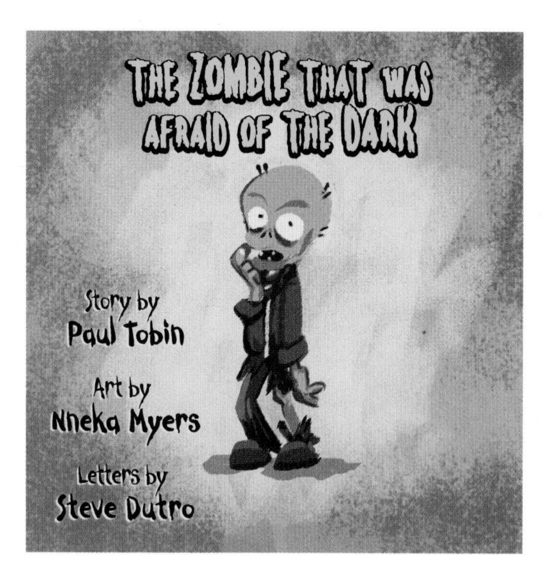
THE ZOMBIE THAT WAS AFRAID OF THE DARK
Story by
Paul Tobin
Art by
Nneka Myers
Letters by
Steve Dutro

EEP!
Once there was a zombie who was afraid of the dark.

He refused to step one foot into the night, because who knew what scary things might be lurking in the darkness?

BRAAAINZZ?
His friends tried to coax him outside with flashlights.

BRAINZ?
They tried to coax him out with candles.

And with one hundred and seventy-two lightning bugs on leashes.

They even tried cattle prods, but nothing seemed to work.
BRAINZ?
TZZZAK
BRAINZ?
BRAINZ?
BRAINZ?
BRAINZ?
BRAINZ?
"What will we do?" his friends asked. "How will we solve this dilemma?" "Whatever can be done?" Or at least they said things that roughly approximated these questions.

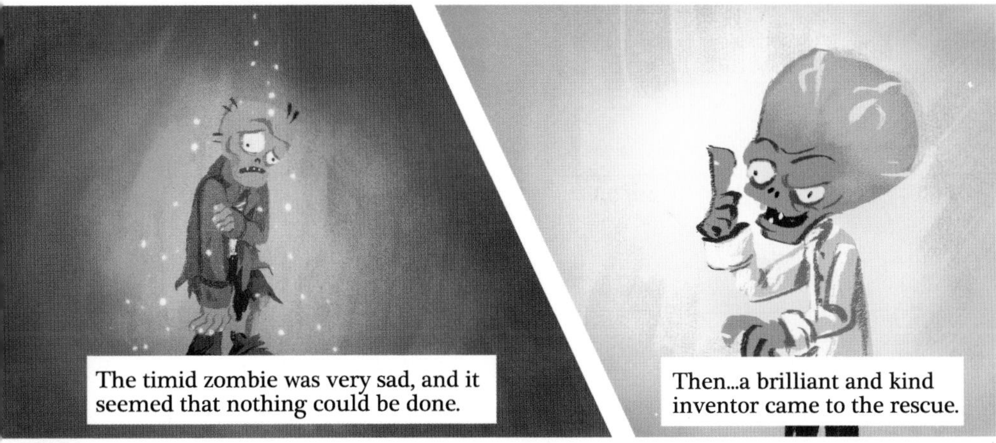
The timid zombie was very sad, and it seemed that nothing could be done.
Then...a brilliant and kind inventor came to the rescue.

He made the zombie a suit of brilliant, glowing white, so that wherever the zombie would go, there would be abundant light.

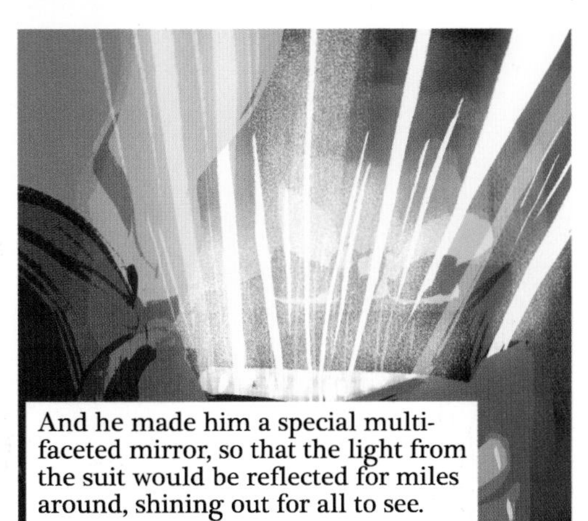
And he made him a special multi-faceted mirror, so that the light from the suit would be reflected for miles around, shining out for all to see.

His friends were amazed!
And he was delighted.

And that, children, is how Disco Zombie was born!

THE END

Know Your Zombie Holidays!
Story: Paul Tobin
Art: Brian Churilla
Letters: Steve Dutro

Shuffle Day is on January 23, commemorating the day when Erastus Zombie first invented shuffling.
CLAP
CLAP
CLAP
CLAP
CLAP
SHUFFLE
SHUFFLE
SHUFFLE

Valenbrainz is on February 14, when an imp in a diaper flies through the air...making everyone very nervous.

FITTING ROOM
The Springening, from March 24 to April 9. All zombies celebrate spring by throwing away last year's clothes and finding a brand-new outfit.

Karaoke Day is July 23.
BRAAAAINS.
BRAINS BRAINS
BRAINZZ
BRAINS BRAINS
BRAINS
BRAAAAINS
BRAINS

Bring a Cat to Work Day is on August 5.
MRAWR!
THP!
MREW!

Worker Appreciation Minute, October 6. Every year, Dr. Zomboss gives his thanks to all the thousands of zombies who serve him. The holiday starts at 12:32 in the afternoon and ends at 12:33 sharp.

Feastivus is from December 24 to December 28, when zombies buy gifts of food for each other...
...but then never exchange gifts and just hoard them for themselves.

And, lastly, there's Brain Year, which takes place from January 1 to December 31 every year.
BRAINZZ.

The end.

The Development of the Balloon Zombie.
ZOMBIE HISTORY vol. 38
Story: Paul Tobin
Art: Brian Churilla
Letters: Steve Dutro

The balloon zombie of today is the noble king of the skies, but what of the years of research that went into the development of this creature of soaring majesty?

Here we see kite zombies, which were considered too impractical, owing to the fickleness of the wind and...

...the tendency of other zombies to forget they were holding on to the strings.
BRAINS?

And who can forget the beanie-propeller zombies?

Or the inflatable zombies?
BRAINZZ?

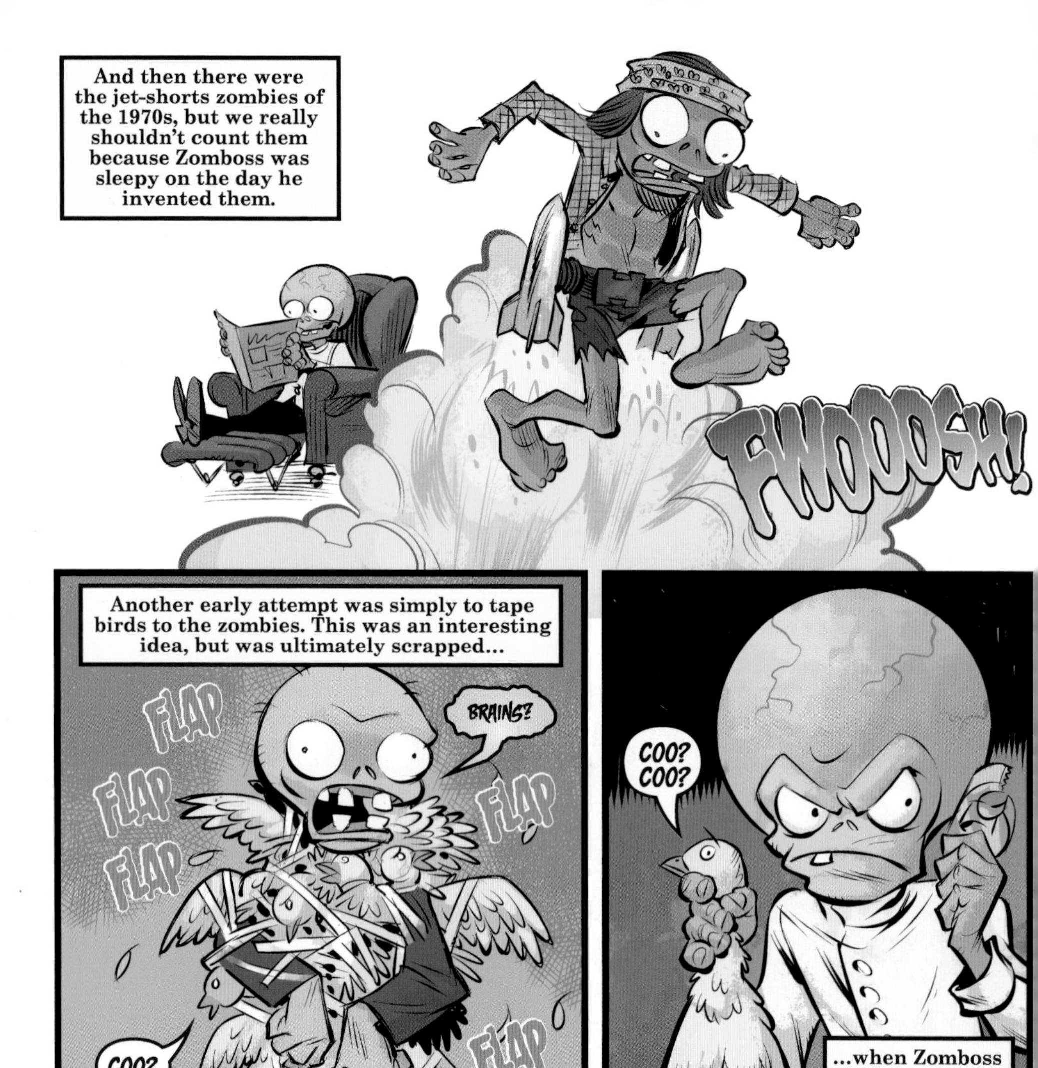
And then there were the jet-shorts zombies of the 1970s, but we really shouldn't count them because Zomboss was sleepy on the day he invented them.
FWOOOSH!
Another early attempt was simply to tape birds to the zombies. This was an interesting idea, but was ultimately scrapped...
FLAP
FLAP
FLAP
BRAINS?
FLAP
FLAP
COO?
COO? COO?
...when Zomboss ran out of tape.

Finally...after years of trial and error and a few years of just simply error...
...we now have this swan of the skies, this king of the clouds, this gallant knight of the airways...

THUNNK
POP!
...the balloon zombie.
The end.

NOISE FROM THE BOYS
Story by Paul Tobin
Art by Cat Farris
Letters by Steve Dutro
FWEEP!

BOOF BOFF BUDDA-DUDDA-DUH
BOOF BOFF

BOOF BOFF
BUDDA-DUDDA-DUH
BOOF BOFF

BANG
HUMP
SMACK
THUMP THUMP

BANG THUMP SMACK
THUMP THUMP

WHAMM
EVER PUNCH
WHACK
WHUMPFF
WHAPP

WHACK THUMP WHAMM
POW! THUD SMACK

WHACK
THUMP
WHAMM
POW!
THUD
SMACK

BOOF BOFF THUD SMACK
THAKK!
GAH! NATE! I NEED YOUR HELP!
POW!

GRRAWRR-BEAR THE ULTIMATE FACE-PUNCHER SPENDS ALL NIGHT ON THAT PUNCHING BAG YOU BOUGHT HIM! I CAN'T SLEEP! DO SOMETHING!
ICE CREAM
OKAY. I GOT THIS. NO PROBLEM.

FIFTEEN MINUTES LATER...

CRAKK!
BOOM BOOM!
WHOMP!
THOOM THOOM!

THOOM
BUMP-A
BUMP-A
BOOM
BANG
KRASH
PATRICE, YOU DON'T NEED TO WORRY ABOUT THAT PUNCHING BAG ANYMORE, BECAUSE...
BOOM
BOOM
BOOM

"...I DISTRACTED HIM WITH A DRUM SET!"
BOOM BOOM!
WHOMP!
BOOM
BANG
KRASH
THOOM THOOM!
BUMP-A BUMP-A
THE END.

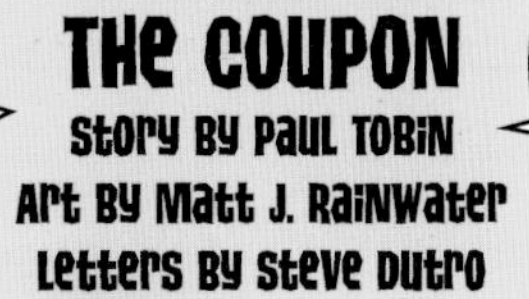
The Coupon
Story by Paul Tobin
Art by Matt J. Rainwater
Letters by Steve Dutro

I...I CAN'T BELIEVE IT. YOU'VE DONE EVERYTHING I ASKED. EVERY JOB HAS BEEN COMPLETED...AND DONE WELL.
MY POP SMARTS ARE TOASTED. YOU RENEWED MY SUBSCRIPTION TO CONQUER MAGAZINE. MY BOWLER HAT HAS BEEN DUSTED...
CONQUER
YODEL

"...AND YOU'VE CALLED MY OLD COLLEGE 10,000 TIMES TO VOTE FOR ME AS THE GREATEST ALUM OF ALL TIME."
Voting For Most Distinguished Alum
FrogPants: 1111
TugBoat: 11
Little Timmy: 1
Mr. Stubbins:
TO SHOW MY... WHAT'S THE WORD...? APPRECIATION...? I'M GOING TO GIVE YOU THIS.
HERE'S A COUPON TO GET YOU OUT OF WORK FOR A FULL DAY. ALL YOU NEED TO DO, WHENEVER YOU WANT A DAY OFF, IS TO HAND THIS TO ME.
GEL

SHUFFLE
RUN
SHUFFLE
RUN
SHUFFLE
RUN

PUTT PUTT
PUTT
SHUFFLE
RUN
SHUFFLE

SHUFFLE
RUN SHUFFLE

SHUFFLE RUN
SHUFFLE

AAAAAAAAA!
EH, WHAT'S THIS?
SHUFFLE
RUN
SHUFFLE

HMM... THIS COUPON HAS EXPIRED.

"GET BACK TO WORK."
THE END.

The Adventures of

AH, SHERLOCK BRAINS! YOU'RE HERE! JOLLY GOOD! I'M AFRAID THERE'S BEEN... A KIDNAPPING!
THE ONLY CLUES LEFT WERE...

...A SET OF FINGER-PRINTS ON THE WINDOWSILL...
POP!

...VIDEO FOOTAGE OF THE ACTUAL KIDNAPPING...

CLINK
CLANK
...THESE MUDDY FOOTPRINTS, WITH THEIR OWNER'S NAME ETCHED INTO THE HEEL...

...AND THIS DROPPED WALLET, WITH IDENTIFICATION CARDS, AN ADDRESS, AND A BLUEPRINT OF THE ENTIRE KIDNAPPING PLAN.
FLIP!
FLAP!
FLIP!
FLAP!

I WAS HOPING THAT YOU, THE GREAT DETECTIVE, COULD USE YOUR INCREDIBLE MENTAL ABILITIES TO SOLVE THIS MYSTERY, EVEN THOUGH THERE'S SO LITTLE FOR US WHEN IT COMES TO CLUES.
SO... SHERLOCK BRAINS...CAN YOU SOLVE THIS?!
FOUR HOURS LATER...
SIX MONTHS LATER...
TWELVE YEARS LATER...
BRAINS?
THE END.

THE ADVENTURES OF
SHERLOCK BRAINS:
THE CASE OF THE
PURLOINED POP SMARTS!
Story: PAUL TOBIN
Art: CHRIS SHERIDAN
Letters: STEVE DUTRO

WHAT? I HAD TWO PLATES OF POP SMARTS! ONE OF THEM'S MISSING!
WHO COULD HAVE STOLEN IT?
WHAT'S THE SOLUTION TO THIS MYSTERY?

MR. STUBBINS! GO FETCH ME SHERLOCK BRAINS...THE ZOMBIE WORLD'S FOREMOST CONSULTING DETECTIVE!
SQUICK!
SCURRY
SCURRY
SCURRY

VRRRTTT!!

AND SOON...
DRAMATIC OPENING!!!

AH, SHERLOCK BRAINS!
IT SEEMS THAT ONE OF MY PLATES OF POP SMARTS HAS GONE MISSING AND...

...AND...
MUNCH
MUNCH
MUNCH
MUNCH MUNCH
AAAAAAAAAA...
HRRG!
MUNCH
MUNCH
MUNCH
TAP
TAP
TAP
MUNCH
THUNNK
BRAAAAAAINS?
HWIP!
THE END.

PAUL TOBIN
(Story)
JEREMY VANHOOZER
(Art)
STEVE DUTRO
(Letters)
Present:
Toasted
URGGH! MY TOASTER... BROKEN??!
FROGPANTS, HAVE YOU BEEN USING IT TO DO YOUR LAUNDRY AGAIN?
FZZT
ZIK
FROWWWNT
ZIK

FROOOGPANTS.

WELL, NO CHOICE...
I NEED MY POP SMARTS, AND UNTIL I FIX MY TOASTER--I'LL HAVE TO TOAST THEM THE OLD-FASHIONED WAY.

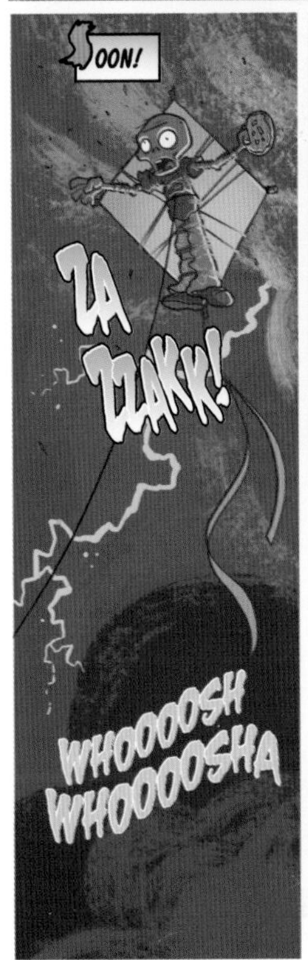
SOON!
ZA ZZAKK!
WHOOOOSH
WHOOOOSHA

BRAINS?

KZZZZZZORK!

ZZT
ZZT
FROOOGPANTSSS...
MMM! THIS IS... PERFECT!
MAYBE I DON'T NEED TO FIX MY TOASTER AFTER ALL!
MUNCH
MUNCH
MUNCH
The end.

THE SCENIC VIEW

STORY: PAUL TOBIN ART: JEREMY VANHOOZER LETTERS: STEVE DUTRO

ICE SCREAM
STORY: PAUL TOBIN
ART: JEREMY VANHOOZER
LETTERS: STEVE DUTRO

PLFAFF GROB-TIME IFFLE-BUTT!

DID YOU JUST SAY...YOU MADE ME AN ICE-CREAM-SEEKING ROBOT?

ice cream find the ice cream find find find
THANKS, UNCLE DAVE!

AND SO, SOON...
This way. This way. This way.
GLOOG GLOOG GLOOG
AND...
This way. This way. This way.
PUTT PUTT PUTT
BRAINS?
POP!
PFOOT

This way. This way. This way.
SUPER FUN PLAYTIME MASKING TAPE

CHOMP CHOMP CHOMP TIME
ICE CREAM
There is ice cream.
There is ice cream.
There is ice cream.
AH, SWEET ICE CREAM!

THIS WAY. THIS WAY. THIS WAY.
SLURP!
MMM!

ICE CREAM ACQUIRED!
HEY! WHAT?
GRAB!

WHAT WAS *THAT* ALL ABOUT?

HEY, PATRICE! *THERE* YOU ARE! I'VE BEEN LOOKING *ALL OVER* FOR YOU!
GUESS *WHAT*...!

YOUR UNCLE MADE ME AN ICE-CREAM-GRABBING ROBOT!
SLURRK!
THE END.

COVER GALLERY

PLANTS VS. ZOMBIES #4
COVER INKS BY ANDIE TONG

PLANTS VS. ZOMBIES #4
COVER COLORS BY ANDIE TONG

PLANTS VS. ZOMBIES #5
COVER INKS BY ANDIE TONG

PLANTS VS. ZOMBIES #5
COVER COLORS BY ANDIE TONG

PLANTS VS. ZOMBIES #6
COVER INKS BY ANDIE TONG

PLANTS VS. ZOMBIES #6
COVER COLORS BY ANDIE TONG

PLANTS VS. ZOMBIES #8
COVER ART BY RON CHAN

PLANTS VS. ZOMBIES #9
COVER ART BY RON CHAN

PLANTS VS. ZOMBIES #10
COVER INKS BY JACOB CHABOT

PLANTS VS. ZOMBIES #10
COVER COLORS BY JACOB CHABOT

PLANTS VS. ZOMBIES #11
COVER INKS BY JACOB CHABOT

PLANTS VS. ZOMBIES #11
COVER COLORS BY JACOB CHABOT

PLANTS VS. ZOMBIES #12
COVER INKS BY JACOB CHABOT

PLANTS VS. ZOMBIES #12
COVER COLORS BY JACOB CHABOT

CREATOR BIOS

Paul Tobin

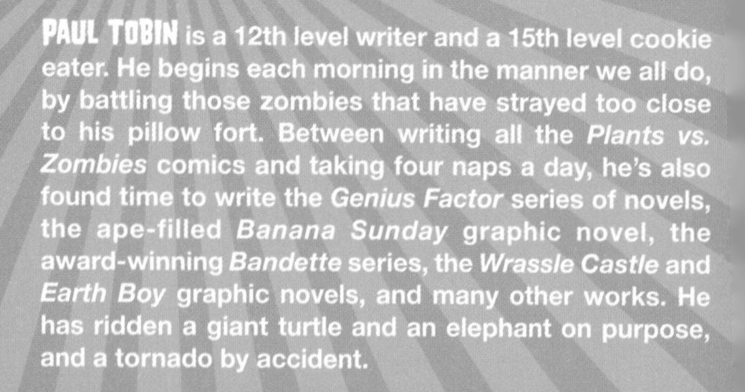

PAUL TOBIN is a 12th level writer and a 15th level cookie eater. He begins each morning in the manner we all do, by battling those zombies that have strayed too close to his pillow fort. Between writing all the *Plants vs. Zombies* comics and taking four naps a day, he's also found time to write the *Genius Factor* series of novels, the ape-filled *Banana Sunday* graphic novel, the award-winning *Bandette* series, the *Wrassle Castle* and *Earth Boy* graphic novels, and many other works. He has ridden a giant turtle and an elephant on purpose, and a tornado by accident.

Ron Chan

RON CHAN is a comic book and storyboard artist, video game fan, and occasional jujitsu practitioner. He was born and raised in Portland, Oregon, where he still lives and works as a member of the local artist collective Helioscope Studio. His comics work has been published by Dark Horse, Marvel, and Image Comics, and storyboarding work includes boards for 3-D animation, gaming, user-experience design, and advertising for clients such as Microsoft, Amazon Kindle, Nike, and Sega. He really likes drawing Bonk Choys. (He also enjoys eating actual bok choy in real life.)

Andie Tong

ANDIE TONG was born in Malaysia, migrated to Australia at a young age, and then moved to London in 2005. In 2012, he journeyed back to Asia and currently resides in Singapore with his wife and children. Andie started off as a multimedia designer in 1997 and migrated to doing comics full time in 2006. Since then he has worked on titles such as *Tron: Betrayal*, *Spectacular Spider-Man*, The Batman Strikes!, Smallville, *The Wheel of Time*, *Tales of the Teenage Mutant Ninja Turtles*, *Masters of the Universe*, *The Legend of Shang-Chi*, and *Green Lantern: Legacy*, working for companies such as Disney, Marvel, DC Comics, Panini, Dark Horse, and Dynamite Entertainment, and has made commercial illustrations for numerous advertising agencies including Nike, Universal, CBS, Mattel, and Hasbro. When he gets the chance, Andie does concept design for various companies and also juggles illustration duties on a range of children's picture storybooks for Harper Collins.

Jacob Chabot

JACOB CHABOT is a New York City-based cartoonist and illustrator. His credits include work for *Sponge-Bob Comics*, *Simpsons Comics*, *Marvel Super Hero Adventures*, *Marvel Tsum Tsum*, *Hello Kitty*, *Strange Tales*, and his own all-ages, Eisner-nominated book *The Mighty Skullboy Army* (published by Dark Horse Comics). Jacob has drawn several *Plants vs. Zombies* graphic novels that you may have read: *Garden Warfare* Volume 1, *Boom Boom Mushroom*, and *The Greatest Show Unearthed*!

Matt J. Rainwater

MATT J. RAINWATER is a freelance illustrator whose work has been featured in advertising, web design, and independent video games. On top of this, he also self-publishes several comic books, including *Trailer Park Warlock*, *Garage Raja*, and *The Feeling Is Multiplied*—all of which can be found at MattJRainwater.com. His favorite zombie-bashing strategy utilizes a line of Bonk Choys with a Wall-nut front guard and Threepeater covering fire.

Steve Dutro

STEVE DUTRO is a pinball fan and an Eisner Award-nominated comic book letterer from Redding, California, who can also drive a tractor. He graduated from the Kubert School and has been lettering comics since the days when foil-embossed covers were cool, working for Dark Horse (*The Fifth Beatle*, *I Am a Hero*, *StarCraft*, *Star Wars*, *Witcher*), Viz, Marvel, and DC Comics. He has submitted a request to the Department of Homeland Security that in the event of a zombie apocalypse he be put in charge of all digital freeway signs so citizens can be alerted to avoid nearby brain-eatings and the like.

DARK HORSE'S FIRST ZOMNIBUS!

Collecting the *New York Times* Best Selling series!

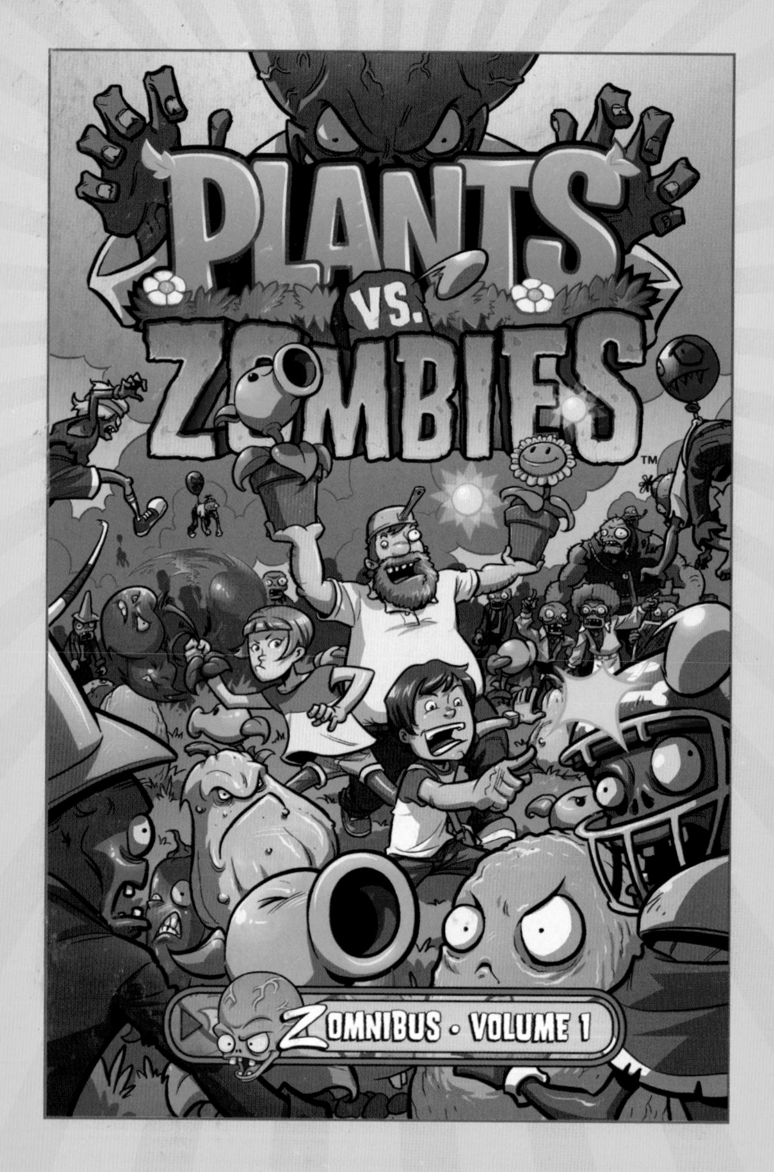

PLANTS VS. ZOMBIES ZOMNIBUS VOLUME 1

ISBN 978-1-50671-415-8

"Very stream of consciousness and prone to bizarre interludes, flashbacks, and shifts in focus."—IGN